SHERIFF AT WATERSTOP

Andy Thomson

journeyforth®

Greenville, South Carolina

Sheriff at Waterstop

Cover and illustrations by Timothy N. Davis and Stephanie True
Edited by Olivia Tschappler

© 1986 by BJU Press
Greenville, South Carolina 29614
JourneyForth Books is a division of BJU Press

Printed in the United States of America

ISBN 978-0-89084-371-0

20   19   18   17   16   15   14

For Lisa Dale Wetzel,
Her kind parents,
And a merry Christmas at the farmhouse

Publisher's Note

This is the story of two men who know the Lord—Micah Huggins and Felix Jensen.

Who is the blond and silent boy who appears on Micah's doorstep? He is the stranger, the suppliant, the fatherless, and the oppressed. Micah, true to his Christian faith, offers shelter and help to this stranger. Micah is the man who has grown up close to the Faith—respectable, kind, devout. He has come to the West seeking work. And then Joseph comes. According to the custom of the West, and operating in the image of Christ, Micah makes the boy his partner—a junior partner, surely, but a fellow worker and a friend.

Felix Jensen is the changed man. He had seldom darkened the door of a church before getting saved at a camp meeting. In his past are shadows which occasionally haunt him, but he is forgiven, and he knows it. He is a man sadder but wiser, yet tough—even tougher than Micah—and equipped with a keen insight of the sinfulness of man. Though fresh from the East, he has a fast draw and a cool head when dealing with desperate men. His courage is based on his faith in God and his unshakable belief that right will always win out in the end.

Felix and his son, Bret, are just getting to know each other in the tough West, and father and son have plenty of room to be pleasantly surprised at each other's courage, honesty, and loyalty. Felix's story is about his forgiveness—how God's forgiveness to him spills over to his circle of Christian family and friends until all that was lost eventually is restored. The quality of forgiving others, difficult for Felix alone, becomes possible when God is the moving force behind it.

Contents

Chapter One
The Surveyor's Cabin

Above a craggy gray mountain, a mother eagle was teaching her young to fly. The four of them circled in the air and then swooped down, rose again, dived again, and on and on.

On the bare face of the mountainside, close to the summit, nestled a cabin made of real boards that had weathered and baked and run their sap in the sun until they were almost the gray-and-mustard color of the stones themselves. On the sagging porch of this bare little cabin, a man sat whittling. Every now and then he turned his attention to the birds above, watched them thoughtfully, and then returned to his work.

At last he stirred himself enough to call out, "Joseph, you ought to come out and see that mama and her eagles. It's a prime sight. How those young'uns are going to land sure beats me."

In answer, a tall, slim boy in homespun shirt and pants came to the door and obediently watched the sky.

"Ain't that the purtiest sight you ever did see?" the man asked. "You can't clap your eyes on something like that just anywhere, now can you, Joseph?" There was no answer, but the man went on in amiable talk, almost as though he were talking to himself. "Now them Injuns, they think the eagles are up there communin' with their spirits. But it's a purty sight just the same, ain't it?"

The boy gave a slight jerk of his head in answer, and the man said, "Say now, quit your chores for a while, Joseph. The place is spick-and-span. See if you can match this from the doorway." And he took his knife in a firmer grip, balanced it for a moment in his hand, and then threw it at one of the corner posts of the porch. "See if you can match it, Joseph."

The boy disappeared into the house and came out after a moment. He had a knife in his hand, but he didn't seem to waste a moment balancing it as his older companion had. There was merely a blur of his hand and a flick of his wrist, and the knife was suddenly embedded an inch or so into the same post, the blade about half an inch from the blade of the first knife.

"You sure do beat all with that!" the man exclaimed. "Well! Since you've licked me again, I guess I'll tote up the water, eh?" And he reluctantly swung his legs down from where they had been perched lazily on the tilting porch rail. He pulled the knives out of the post, which was already decorated with many knife cuts from previous contests, and handed the boy's weapon back to him, sheathing his own and shambling down the path to the pump.

He was not an old man—scarcely thirty yet, though the wrinkles around his eyes and on his forehead spoke of years spent out in the wilderness exposed to the sun and wind. Under his battered Stetson hat with its roomy crown and wide brim, he had a thick and slightly matted shock of brown hair that he kept crammed down under the hat in place of combing it. He had a week's growth on his chin and cheeks. But his clothes were reasonably clean and fairly new—workshirt and jeans and well-heeled boots that looked recently bought. His leather belt was polished and smooth, not cracked and faded.

The pump was a few yards from the house—a situation he did not like, for his mind often turned to Indians and the problem of renegades who might one day sight the smoke from his cabin and come for a visit. As a general rule the Indians were calm these days and had been persuaded to stay on the reservations, but the truth was that, in addition to the larger tribes who had once roamed these canyons and mountains in search of wild horses and scattered grasslands, there had been numerous smaller tribes perhaps yet unknown to the white men. And even aside from the smaller tribes and half-tribes, there were the renegades.

All the same, the pump and cabin had been there before he had come, and so he had been obliged to make do. And so far, the Indians had been no problem.

After pumping out a bucketful of water, he walked back to the cabin, more slowly now so as not to spill a drop. A man alone in the hills played these little games constantly, he had noticed—trying to walk without spilling water, setting time limits on his chores, racing himself, challenging himself whenever possible in order to maintain some control over the vast and unbroken silences that settled down over the mustard-colored hills.

Of course it was not so urgent now, not with Joseph for company. He entered the threshold of the cabin, kicked his boots one after another against the doorjamb to knock off the dust, and entered with the water. The boy was at the store-bought stove, getting ready to fish out some of the white beans from the simmering pot to add to the jerked beef that would be softened and cooked as much as possible.

"Vittles has become a lot better since you been here," the man admitted while he hunted up the tin plates and forks and brought out a handful of old dried biscuits from a big sealed tin where they stored their bread.

Joseph glanced at him appreciatively. "Gotta get good meat soon," he said.

"Feel like huntin' when the time comes?" the man asked, pulling a greasy and tarnished watch from his pants pocket and winding it. "Be a few months yet before the time is right for a fat antelope down below. But it might be nice to get away from here awhile, huh?"

He was undisturbed when Joseph did not pursue the conversation. Weeks ago he had discovered that Joseph was a silent but agreeable companion who seldom spoke but liked being spoken to, and he was fond of thinking that if more people had been made that way, there'd be a lot less trouble in the world.

Chapter Two
A Visitor

Micah Huggins had been a surveyor for the railroads before the lure of big gold stakes had taken him up into the high ranges of the Rocky Mountains. Big gold stakes he had found indeed, along with double loads of buckshot from men who didn't want to share hidden finds and secret lodes with anybody. Moreover, he had also been chased off the ranges and threatened with brandings from disgruntled cowhands who could already see the sun setting on the days of the wide open cattle ranges.

Indians he had met, both friendly and hostile, but he understood them little, and frankly admitted it to himself. Their hunting grounds had sprawled across huge strips of the West—lengthwise strips that had now been cut and crisscrossed by the merciless iron rails of the trains. The sun was also setting on their days of freedom and glory.

But since he didn't care for buckshot or arrows coming in his direction, he had retired to this bit of broken rock where he commanded a view of the lower ranges. He had enough gold stored up in his bags to enable him to live for several years in his retreat, only occasionally venturing lower to hunt or to make necessary trips to the sparse settlements that called themselves towns. A circuit rider had discovered the cheer of his cabin in a rainstorm a year before. He returned every couple of months to preach a sermon or two and share the usual fare of beef and beans that Micah could offer, along with a dried apple pie cooked up special for company.

Other than the preacher's visits, Micah had been alone for the first fifteen months of his retreat, and he had spent most of his time ranging around, prospecting for bits of gold or panning for it where it showed up here and there in the streams. There was never enough for a man to get rich, not like the big claims, but there was some to be found just the same, plenty to satisfy a man of few wants. And then Joseph had come.

The boy had appeared one morning as a mute appeal for help, for he had stood speechless in Micah's doorway, startling the man at his breakfast.

Micah's exclamation of surprise at having a visitor must have sounded like a roar, and the boy had vanished as quickly as he'd come. But Micah had called him back, called with so much fear in his voice that he had even startled himself at his tone. It was fear for the boy, alone in these inhospitable hills. But the boy had come back at the call, and they became friends.

Micah had named him after Joseph in the Bible because the boy had come, he figured, from far away and had apparently been sold or given to folks who had been cruel to him. Slavery, though now illegal in all the states of the Union and her territories, still existed among the Indians in some places as a punishment for captives. The nearest that Micah could figure was that Indians had killed the boy's family or simply carried him off and then enslaved him or sold him to somebody else. In any case, for a name the boy would only mumble some unpronounceable Indian title given him at one time, and since he didn't seem to mind, Micah called him Joseph.

They sat down to their meal of beef, beans, and hard bread, washing it down with the pump water Micah had toted in. After they had eaten, Micah cleared the plates away, poured some of the water from the bucket into a basin, and washed the few tin utensils and dishes while Joseph put coffee on the stove. After the coffee was done and Joseph had sweetened his from the dwindling supply of molasses, they went out onto the porch again, seating themselves on the crates that doubled as chairs, and pulled out their knives.

Micah threw first at the post, and then Joseph threw, once again getting his blade within an inch of Micah's. Then Micah pulled the knives down, and Joseph threw first, followed by Micah, who still had to hesitate to aim. His knife also came close, but not nearly so close as Joseph's had been on the first throw. After a few more matches at the post, Micah and Joseph put up their knives and drank their cooled coffee.

Evening shadows spilled down from the cabin across the path leading up to the porch. Down in the valley, purple and blue-gray shadows were shawled around the trees like winter wraps. The shadows would creep up the mustard-colored hill and gradually envelop the cabin and pump, and the two partners would turn in for the night.

But that night Joseph suddenly sat up a little straighter and listened, and in a moment Micah heard it too—hoofbeats. Without a word he stood up, ready to duck inside and get his gun if need be. Seconds later a rider had crested the top of the path. A rider appeared, dressed all in somber black that made Joseph stiffen, but the man called, "Hallo the cabin! Anybody there?"

"Sure 'nuff, Preacher!" Micah called. "Come on in and set right up. You hungry?"

"No, I had a bite back on the trail." Preacher reigned up at the porch and swung off the horse with the grace

7

born of a cowboy who has ridden the ranges. He pushed back his broad-brimmed hat and looked at Joseph. "Well, who might you be?"

"That there's Joseph," Micah said. "My partner."

When Preacher extended his hand Joseph shook it, and Micah gave a little smile of approval.

The Preacher was tall and thin, a little over thirty, with brown eyes and neat, short brown hair that was thinned out quite a bit up on top. Despite his premature baldness, he was handsome. His beard was short and well-trimmed.

He threw himself down onto a crate.

"What's the news?" Micah asked.

"Oh, not much, I guess. Those folks at the bottom of Bald Mountain gave it up and went to Dodge to get the first train back East."

"Well, they been talkin' about it for a while," Micah said.

"Yup. West ain't for everybody. Gets mighty solitary out here, doesn't it?" Preacher asked.

"Sure 'nuff. Could drive a man batty if it didn't drive him back East," Micah agreed. "What'd they do with those shorthorn they'd invested in?"

"Sold 'em to the Lazy E. Some of their men were going through, and they bought up the stock cheap."

"Lazy E? That's a piece up the trail, ain't it?"

"Yup. Up at Waterstop. Well, like you said, it sure does get solitary out here," Preacher concluded.

Micah cocked an eye at the tall man, who was stretched out in comfort on the crate with his back against the planks of the cabin.

"I reckon we'd agreed on that a'ready, Preacher," he said.

"Sometimes I wonder why you stick it out around here," Preacher added carelessly. "There can't be much gold up here, eh?"

"Not a lot, that's for sure, or we'd be crawling with horse thieves, whiskey, gambling, and all the rest," Micah replied. "I reckon I like the solitude better."

"Not every town's got those problems, Micah, and it does get mighty lonely up here."

"Not with my partner Joseph here. Say, Preacher, what are you driving at? You know I'm a God-fearing man what tends to his own work."

"That's what I'm gettin' at. I hear tell the folks at Waterstop are in need of a sheriff. I'd like to get 'em a decent man that can't be bought and doesn't hold with liquor."

Micah gave a snort of laughter and surprise. "Sure 'nuff I don't hold with that stuff, but a sheriff's gotta shoot good too, like his life depends on it, which it does most times, I reckon. And I can't shoot that good—not with a Colt. When you hear me slap leather, it'll be my boots slappin' the ground, beatin' it out of the way of a gunfight."

He was interrupted by the horse, who jangled his bit to turn and look at Joseph. The slim boy had come over to pet the animal and offer it a sticky handful of coffee-soaked molasses from the bottom of his cup.

"Wanna ride him, Joseph?" Preacher asked. "You can if you want."

Joseph nodded, took the reins, and suddenly flung himself atop the saddle without touching the stirrups. He took the horse off in a canter around the front of the cabin.

"That boy's learnt from an Indian," Preacher observed. "Where'd you pick him up?"

"He picked me up," Micah said. "Just showed up one day lookin' hungry and alone, so I made him my partner. You ever seen him before?"

"Not that I recall. Look at him go, Micah! He's ridden before, and not just with Indians. He's got some cow-punching under his belt."

"Him? He's a kid."

"Hmm." Preacher knit his eyebrows and frowned.

"Seemed clear to me he's been with Indians," Micah added, "but he come to me wearin' white men's clothes, and he cooks right good, and in the fashion of white men."

"Good hand at cookin', is he?"

"Yup. Right good. Just took right over fixing up vittles for the both of us."

"They use boys at cow camps sometimes."

"Reckon so? Could be the Indians sold him out to men on a cattle drive or ranch somewheres. They'd a been glad of an extra hand to help, I reckon."

Joseph was riding back, shaggy blond hair flying, face fixed in a grin at the freedom he felt on the horse's back.

"He's a high rider, isn't he?" Preacher asked. "Looks like a squire just stepped out of *Ivanhoe*."

Micah nodded and smiled. He had read and reread the book by Sir Walter Scott. It was popular in the civilized sections of the country, and copies had drifted out to the West in the saddlebags of wandering men who sought companionship in a written word.

The boy reigned up and swung off. "Good horse!" he exclaimed and threw himself back onto his chair.

Chapter Three
Joseph's Good-bye

There wasn't any excitement after the Preacher left. He had extended his stay to make friends with Joseph and to preach a couple of sermons to the congregation of two in the tiny cabin. There had been endless talk about this family and that, this ranch or that buyer, this crook who had at last met his end, or such-and-such a lawman who was at last cleaning up a town on the frontier so that decent folks could come in.

Preacher had left a shorter catechism for Micah to read to Joseph, since the boy was mostly unlettered, and had departed down the steep trail to continue his circuit. He would spread word that Micah had taken on an orphan boy who'd been raised by Indians awhile and then given or sold to cattlemen to work as a cook's boy, or mariann. Preacher was Micah's only connecting thread to civilization, and he was a slight thread, for the safety of circuit riders was often in jeopardy and the circuits were long. Micah had no idea when he would return.

The leaves down below turned color. They now presented a riot of orange and yellow patches mixed with the deep greens of the fir trees, and Joseph's eyes would follow the colors as though tracing trails of brilliance in a pool of green.

It was time to go to town. Micah had lost his horse in a flash flood while he had been on a prospecting tour. He meant to make the long trip with Joseph on foot, and then purchase a couple of horses for their use.

Winter on the bare, bald face of the mountain was depressing and harsh. He knew about various cabins and stopovers located here and there in more sheltered places, and he wondered about wintering in a less hostile spot.

He still hadn't made the decision when the time came for them to make their packs and prepare for the long trip on the morrow. That morning as they cleaned the only two rifles Micah owned and counted the ammunition, Micah again heard hoofbeats outside on the rock-bedded path. He went to the door, rifle held casually in his hand. Curious, Joseph watched through a crack in the shutters.

A lean, hard-looking man came riding up the path. He wore wide leather chaps and a pistol on his hip, and he was leading a spare horse. A rifle sheath and rifle were on his own saddle, which also sported a bedroll, as did the saddle of the horse with him.

"Hello the cabin!"

"Come up," Micah called, and the man walked his horse up to the rail.

"Heard tell from a preacher down a ways about a boy you got up here."

"Me and my partner live here, all right."

"Reckon he's about fifteen or sixteen if he's the boy I'm looking for."

"Well, my partner's a young kid," Micah admitted, but without any hint of giving in. For some reason he dreaded this lean young man who eyed everything with the carelessness of a cowpuncher who's been on too many trails. But he wasn't afraid of him.

"I had an aunt and uncle comin' out this way 'bout ten years ago," the man said. "Name of Stewart. Come by wagon train, but they got stopped by sickness and then Injuns. Most everybody got killed, but a coupla' the folks that survived tell me my cousin Ned got taken off by Injuns, and I heard that boy you got was raised by Injuns. That right?"

"Indians have took plenty of kids in their time, I guess," Micah said.

"Not so many as a man might think, and not nearly as many around here. Them Injuns that massacred that wagon train hightailed it into these here mountains, mister. Now I'd like to see that partner of yours, if you don't mind."

Micah kept one eye on the stranger as he leaned back inside and said, "Joseph, you want to show yourself?"

And Joseph nodded and came out. The stranger eyed him from the horse, and Joseph looked back at him.

"Well, Ned, I've had a hard time finding you, boy, but here I am, and I aim to send you back to the folks that'll care for you."

Micah wondered if the silent boy would even bother to give answer to the stranger, but to his surprise Joseph gave a brief nod of assent.

"You got any belongings?" the stranger asked. And the boy turned to go in and get his few personal belongings. For a moment Micah Huggins stood like a man stands when an Indian lance has transfixed him, and then he followed Joseph, forgetting about the cowboy.

"Joseph, is that who you really are?" he asked.

The boy said nothing as he hunted around on a shelf for his knife and sheath.

For once Micah couldn't bear the silence, and he broke it. "Don't go with him unless you're sure!"

The boy began to put the belt on. "My parents died when I was young. My first name was Ned, before I got my Indian name," he said. "Now I'll be Ned again." It was more words than he had ever strung together before, and Micah saw that the boy, though he kept his face somber and staid as the Indians had taught him, had been greatly moved at hearing his real name again. Now was his chance to return to anything that was left of his family. And Micah, realizing that it was the boy's right, raised no more objections.

They went back out into the autumn sunlight and the cold shade of the porch. Joseph, or Ned as he was now called, stepped off the sagging porch and patted the spare horse's nose a moment. Then he swung up, Indian style.

Micah had disappeared inside the cabin for a second, but he came back with a small sack in one hand—the results of a long month's toil some years back at a mountain stream. He handed the pouch of gold dust up to the boy. "Maybe this'll tide you over in some tough place, Joseph. Ain't much, somewhere between a hundred and two hundred dollars, but it might help. It might even get you a train ticket back to your people and a set of clothes. But I reckon if you ever need your friend Micah, you can leave word with someone to tell Preacher along the way." Then he thrust up his hand for the boy to take. "Good-bye, partner."

Joseph took the offered hand and shook it. "Good-bye, partner."

The cowboy turned his horse's head and called back. "We're going to Waterstop for a spell until I get enough to send me along with the boy back East to my folks." Then he clucked to the horse and he and Joseph picked their way down the trail.

"They still need a sheriff there?" Micah called back.

"Nah—been a sheriff there for a solid month!"

Glum and defeated, Micah leaned against the porch rail and flipped his knife at the post. It missed.

Chapter Four
The Story of Felix Jensen

If the Great Northern Railroad hadn't needed a waterstop up the line from Cheyenne on one of its branches, there's a good chance that Waterstop might never have come into being. All the families, as well as the wheelwright, blacksmith, and other tradesmen that make a town, would have fanned out in their separate directions and been absorbed into the other growing towns up in the shorthorn country of the new territory of Wyoming.

As it stood, there was a Waterstop, with its main street and little businesses, a small church, and even a school. And there were the outlaws with their fast-barking Colt .45s and the smooth-talking men who were trying to weasel their way in as town bosses and wanted to control the outlaws.

But the law had to come to Waterstop. How would free crime and vigilante justice be stopped? By a sheriff— and a good one, too.

Felix Jensen had ridden broke into the little town. One horse was lame, and the wagon itself was in bad shape from all the way it had come, through mountains and plains, on its way West.

Jensen had brought his wife and son into the town to try to find some supplies on credit and maybe a job somewhere. His clothes were homespun, betraying his heritage of the hills of North Carolina, and his boots were down at the heel and patched in places. He had the hungry, bone-weary look of a man who had lost everything on his trek out to the West. He was instantly marked for prey by one of the toughs who hung around the livery stable where Jensen went in to ask for a piece of work to tide himself and his family over.

"Ain't no handouts in there for you, drifter," the cowboy said to Jensen. "Get going."

"I'm not looking for handouts," Jensen mumbled and pushed past, bent on going in and irritated at being insulted.

A boot tripped him as he went past, and he went face first in the dirt, but he got up and made to keep going. He had promised himself, his wife, and the Lord that he would not be a brawler. He had come out West to put all that behind him, and he would not go back to it.

So he stood up to go in, and just before the man swung at him, he realized that it was different out here. Out here a man would be branded as a coward and hounded the rest of his days if he did not fight back.

He made his choice in time to duck under the awkwardly swung fist, and then he pumped an uppercut into his attacker's chin, hoped that it would be enough to settle him, and once again made to go back inside.

Of course by this time a small crowd had gathered, both from the street and from the livery stable, and when Jensen turned to go inside the stable, he swung around into the faces of about five men, all with mouths open, astonished that he was leaving a fight just when he'd gotten the upper hand.

"Watch out!" they all yelled, and Jensen had the sense to sidestep a blow that grazed the back of his ear, and then he swung a roundhouse into the man's ribs with enough force to wind the attacker and dump him a second time onto the hard-packed ground.

Jensen backed up inside the loose ring of men and this time waited for any other attacks. All the other men ogled the fallen attacker, and Jensen began to get the uneasy feeling that he had just fought somebody "big" in the way of town toughs. Then the man reached for his wide belt, and if somebody hadn't yelled, "He's going for his gun!" it would have been all over for Felix Jensen.

Before the man could slip the thong off his hammer and draw, Jensen had him covered with a Colt .45 drawn out of his waistband and hidden under his vest. The man stopped dead. Jensen had no idea that a fight could lead so quickly to a shooting, but he didn't waste time figuring it out.

"Someone get the sheriff," Jensen said, keeping his attacker covered.

"Ain't no sheriff in Waterstop, mister," one of the spectators said. "We just send the folks we don't like packin' if we get the upper hand on 'em."

"Okay then, you get on your feet, mister, and let down that gunbelt real slow and easy," Jensen said. "And then you get yourself out of town on the double. Your horse in here?" And he jerked his thumb back toward the stable.

"Yup," one of the men put in. "I b'lieve I'll do everyone a favor and get it saddled for him."

Within minutes the man was on his horse and on his way back to whatever ranch he had ridden in from, and Felix Jensen found himself surrounded with new friends.

"That there was Smiley—what's his first name?"

"Jim Smiley!" another man replied. "Mean as any cougar that ever stalked a doe. And you whipped him good! Yessir! But good! If you don't mind my saying, mister, you don't look like much, but you shape up quite a bit in a fight."

"I been in a lot of fights where I come from, but I don't—"

"Say, how about a drink?" one of them asked. "I'll buy for you—"

"No thanks, I'm not partial to saloons."

"Well, don't that beat everything. All the same, maybe you'd like a job here," another said.

It was just what he'd been worrying about and praying for, and Jensen told himself that no matter what kind of menial job they offered him, he would take it.

"Sure!" he exclaimed. "What kind of job?"

"Well, sheriff, what else?"

"But—"

"You handled that gun like a regular wild west show," the man added.

"But I don't—well, I ought to think about it first," Jensen said, remembering that there wasn't a thing left to eat in the wagon except old bread. "But let me ask you this—think the storekeep will let me get vittles on credit? I mean to get some kind of a job, and—"

"Sure, sure, come on in. We'll back you up to him," and the whole group trailed him across the dusty street again and into the store marked FULLER'S GROCERIES AND SUPPLIES.

And that was how Felix Jensen became the sheriff of Waterstop.

Chapter Five
The Sheriff's Wife

"Seems kinda' like the Lord just throwed it into our hands," Felix Jensen observed to his wife as they cleaned their supper dishes in the cool water by the campfire.

Bret, lying up in the wagon and trying to go to sleep, heard the conversation. Perhaps he should have joined in, he told himself. Coming out West, hauling the wagon over waves of grass, and pushing it through sloughs of mud shoulder-to-shoulder with his father had made him much more of a second man in the family, and he knew it. He felt the respect and the glow of friendship in his Pa's eyes when they talked out the troubles on the trails that lay ahead. It was such a new feeling—respect from Pa.

But he promised himself that just this once, just tonight, he would say nothing. For one thing, it would hurt Ma. Bret had seen his father fight the man at the livery stable. He wanted Pa to be sheriff, and it might make Ma cry if they both agreed on that when she didn't like it. Might make her feel left out—and after all they had gone through together, too. It was so important to feel united—so important to pull together. It hadn't always been that way.

His mind replayed the events of the last six months: the camp meeting back in the hills of North Carolina when

he had glimpsed his father standing half-embarrassed and half-defiant in the smoky haze under the oil lamps—in the back, of course—but present to hear the preacher nonetheless.

And Bret had been present at the mourner's bench when Brother Tanner had said, "Bret, Mrs. Jensen, your husband has something he wants to say to you now."

It had been a first that night, when Pa had embraced him and said he was sorry—sorry for everything, and in the darkness Bret blushed when he remembered how the hard hug had been uncomfortable, how he had been a little angered at his father's sobbing breath in his face, at being expected to forgive the man who had brought such shame to him.

It had only been after the time had passed—after he had seen with his own eyes the whiskey still destroyed there by the creek and the bottles and jugs hurled off Tabletop Cliff—that he had dared to believe that salvation and a changed life could come to a man like Felix Jensen. And in the following weeks he had seen his father, without prompting from Ma, read the Bible for himself, leave off his brawling and cussing, and begin to think about making a new life for himself and his family out West, where there would be peace from his past as a moonshiner.

And yet—for a moment Bret resisted the thoughts of doubt, but then he gave in to them again. He knew Pa— knew him inside and out: the hot temper, the quick fists, the impatience—these things had not been so apparent lately, but were they really gone? Or someday, in some unguarded moment, would he once again walk in on one of Pa's rages?

Maybe Pa had looked like an ordinary drifter to that cowpoke by the livery stable, Bret thought. But Felix Jensen had cut his teeth on danger and trouble, and it was pretty certain that once Pa started to fight back, he would win. Whenever Pa met trouble, he sent it back marked with a bill of sale.

Bret rolled restlessly in his blankets in the wagon, heedless of the creaking it made. Ma and Pa were still sitting at the fire and talking. Pa's voice sounded almost apologetic. ". . . know I wanted to be a preacher, Nance, but we both know I never did get a call from the Lord for it, and I don't have an education for it."

"Brother Tanner hasn't been to seminary."

"No, but he's read a good deal of the Scriptures, and I haven't yet. And besides, nobody says I gotta be sheriff forever—and Nance, I feel called. I don't know how else to explain it to you."

"But the saloon, Felix. What about that? You'll have to go into the saloon!"

"Every lawman's got to bust up trouble in the saloons when it comes, just like he busts it up anywhere else he finds it. And I reckon back East there's policemen who have to walk into bars and taverns and pubs and do the same thing. Well, if the Lord would have me to do it, I will. After all, I never did drink much of that poison myself, Nance, not like the people I sold it to. It was the money that had ahold of me—not the liquor. You know that."

"Oh, but Felix, it's not like what you read in the papers and the little dime novels. There's men in that town that have killed people. Are you going to drive them out? You? Alone?"

"I reckon a man can do anything God wants him to do, Nance. And somebody's got to do it."

"But it doesn't have to be you."

"Now look here. You and I wanted to come West where we could find a decent place to live and live like decent folks again—like it was before I built my still. But I don't reckon we got a right to find a decent place and just move in. If a person believes in living decent, Nance, he might just have to make a place decent. If Christian folks want to live where there's law and order, then some of them Christian folks have got to be the law and order. We can't let other people do all the dangerous work while we set back at ease."

"But being a sheriff is a gunfighter's job."

"Nance, those people are mighty good judges of gun-slinging, I guess. And they figure I stand up to the measure about as good as 'most anybody. And what's more, they asked me to help them. And what's even more, they advanced us some grub and gave some relief to old Becky there, who's just about ready to go lame from that poor shoeing she got. If it was just a job offer, honey, I would turn it down for your sake, but it's more than that. It's a cry for help, and I think I got to answer it." He was silent, and then he added, "Besides, they got a church here, Nance. I know the Preacher's gone most of the time, but at least we're on his circuit, and that means real church services about every six weeks. You know we both wanted that."

Ma let out a sigh—the sigh she gave when she knew someone else was in the right, but she was worried and tired. Bret had heard that sigh often in the last few months. Coming West had been hard on her, but she tried not to complain. He heard Pa slide over to her to put his arm around her.

"See them stars up there, honey? That sky's so vast that nobody's ever counted up them stars, and God knows them all by name. And He knows us by name, and He knows we're beat out and tired and maybe a little afraid. But I think if He gives me a tin star, He'll take care of all the rest that goes with it."

Then there was quiet again, except for crickets and the snapping and popping of the campfire. The stillness and the sense of peace at last seeped into Bret. He made himself forget about Pa's past and think instead about the future. A pleasant thrill ran through him. Sheriff! Pa would be a sheriff.

And maybe when I get to be seventeen, and things go well with him, he'll make me deputy, he thought.

Chapter Six
Keeping the Law

THERE ARE TO BE NO GUNS
WORN IN THE SALOON.
ALL FIREARMS ARE TO BE HUNG UP
AT THE DOOR—Sheriff Jensen

It was a good thing Waterstop already had a jail left over from the days when the vigilantes of the town had imprisoned outlaws. Bret had an idea that pretty soon the three barred cells would be filling up, especially after his father posted the notices in the saloon and on the porch posts all over town.

But the first day of his official duties was pretty peaceful. The town had advanced them enough money to rent a little house on the end of Main Street, and nobody minded that Pa spent a good deal of the day unloading their gear and helping Ma get everything set down right. The town council had given him a gun, too, a six-shooter worn in a holster just below his hip; and it was tied down around his thigh—a nuisance, he called it. Bret noticed that Pa continued to wear his slightly long vest with the spare six-shooter stuffed into his waistband. He was more comfortable with that.

But then the afternoon shadows grew longer, and the businesses began closing up for the day.

"Don't wait supper for me, Nance," Pa said. "I reckon it's gonna be a long night." And he went out the door, pausing only to jam his frayed and worn felt hat on his head. He didn't look like a western man; he didn't look like a gunslinger or even like a sheriff, though he wore the star on his vest. Bret thought he looked only like a man from down South. But Bret had seen him whip out his gun and beat a cowboy to the draw, and he prayed that Pa would stay just as fast and clever.

"Come on now, son," Ma said, surveying their spare and worn-down furniture in the sitting room. "At least the kitchen is cozy. Let's fix some supper out of the provisions Pa got. We can't sit and stew, and he told me if we were to do anything it had to be to pray for him after we've eaten. Search me out a two-quart pan, will you? I can set on some beans for tomorrow night, too."

He obeyed her, and helped her prepare their generous supper. Even though Pa had told her not to wait anything for him, she fixed him a separate plate of beef, biscuit, and johnnycake and put it, wrapped in a clean cloth to stay warm, on the very back of the stove. Then they said their blessing and ate, but the whole while they were listening.

They washed up their plates and things and, still listening, went into the sitting room. Ma brought down the big Bible and began reading out loud, but Bret was listening to the street more than he was to her. The few times he forced himself to concentrate, he realized that Ma was getting distracted from the words at every little noise.

"How I wish we were still on the trail," she said at last, and closed the Book. Then she roused herself. "No, Pa was right. Let's just pray for him, Bret. It's a hard thing when a man and a stranger is called upon to clean up a town, even a little town like this."

And she bowed her head and was silent.

Bret meant to pray, but his mind went to Pa and seemed more set on wondering and worrying than on praying. The day had been long and hard, and their supper had been very good. He seemed to be dreaming that Pa was standing on the plank sidewalk telling cowpokes to check their guns inside the door, and all the cowpokes were laughing at his felt hat and just ignoring him, and Bret was pleading to himself, "Don't push them, and don't get mad, Pa. Don't push them, don't—"

Then suddenly he caught himself with a jerk and looked wildly around the room.

"Did you fall asleep, son?" Ma asked.

"I reckon. Pa's not back yet?"

"No. I heard shots about a half hour ago, but there hasn't been a noise since, and Pa told me not to go outside the house tonight no matter what. Surely if something had happened—"

"They'd come get us right off," Bret assured her. But he wondered if anybody in that town would even remember that the new sheriff had a family. They were silent for a long time, and Bret realized that she had bowed her head again. He was about to when the door opened, and Pa stepped in. It was so sudden and quiet that neither of them knew what to do and just sat there, looking at him.

"You two fall asleep?" Pa asked.

Then Ma stood up quickly. Bret followed.

"What happened?" she asked. "We heard shooting."

"Just some cowboys kicking up fun in the street. I directed them on the shortest way out of town, and they went back to their camp. It isn't so bad. Most people don't hanker after a serious shooting against a tin star, Nance. They know it would only take such a thing to stir up a little vigilante justice and roust out the whole countryside."

"These are perilous days," Ma lamented.

Pa smiled and threw his arm around her. Then he clapped his other hand on Bret's shoulder. "It's a glorious country! And it's opening up for all the poor and hard-working people to come and make a new start. There's nothing like this country, I tell you! Where all a man needs is strong hands and a plow to make his way. Nance, once this sheriffing is over, we could get us a little ranch or a farm somewhere and leave it for Bret and our grand-children." He smiled at her, his eyes shining, and then said, "Well, you two get to bed. I figure you left something for me to eat even though I told you not to bother."

Chapter Seven
A Month Later

"Now there's a real sheriff for you," Doc Chesterton said, admiring the dull gleam of Pa's new boots and his high-sitting Stetson hat. "And you too, Bret. You look ready to take on some rustlers, all right."

"Sorry to disappoint you, Doc," Pa laughed. "Me and my boy have been lookin' up the brands together, and we're going out to check the herds comin' to meet the train."

It had been a fast month since they'd settled at Waterstop, and by now the figure of Sheriff Jensen was as familiar and comfortable as the faded front of Fuller's Grocery Store. Far down on the end of Main Street, on the side opposite their little house, the tracks led past the town and out onto the sweeping grasses that ran to meet the distant mountains. The depot was at that end of town, and just in the last few weeks the people had been hurriedly setting up cattle chutes. The town council had somehow arranged to make Waterstop a pickup point for beef being shipped east to Chicago.

The business was a boon to the little town, and several people had an eye on making a tidy profit from putting up cattle dealers, cowboys, and ranchers. A bank had been started, headed up by a college boy who had come West right after getting his sheepskin.

"Fifty to a hundred ranch hands and their bosses'll likely spell trouble in the town tonight," Pa said, removing the big hat long enough to wipe the sweat from his forehead. "But I reckon we'll settle that when tonight comes. Right now we better make sure that everybody's steers are staying in the right camps."

"You gonna' deputize anyone?" Bret asked.

"For tonight? Well, it's a right good suggestion, son. I reckon maybe I will. Fuller said I could count on him, and I reckon Nels the blacksmith will be willing and a good hand to have on my side if there's any fights."

"What about Bill Barton?"

"What, the saloonkeeper? I'd be a ninnyhammer to deputize him. Almost all of the trouble that comes to this town comes because of whiskey, Bret. If Barton wants to help clean up this town, he can start by closing down his bar. And he can finish by leavin' those young cowboys alone instead of gettin' 'em involved in those all-night card games at the ranch houses he visits."

That closed the subject for Pa. Bret looked down, feeling a little rebuked at Pa's tone. But Bill Barton was always pushing to be deputized whenever he thought trouble might be afoot, and he didn't like it when Pa turned him down. Twice in the first month that Pa had been sheriff, Pa had crossed Barton's name off the list of men that the council had given him as likely deputies or volunteers.

Twice Doc Chesterton had asked him why, and twice Pa had insisted that the business of whiskey should never be hand in hand with the business of keeping the law. They thought he was crazy to believe such a thing in a region where very often the sheriff was also judge, jury, and saloonkeeper rolled into one. But since Pa was sheriff and a right good one, they let him have his way.

Pa and Bret rode out of the limits of the town to the cattle camps. Everything seemed quiet. The herds would intermix, but the brands were all registered and of a clean, honest type, not the kind that's been made so that it will fit over any other brand, such as a boxed E or the like. With everybody owning a distinct brand, it would be easy to separate the herds for the cattle buyers.

The sun was beginning to set when they turned their horses back toward the town.

"You're a right smart hand to have along, son," Pa said. "Let's ride on back to your Ma. She'll be having a good supper waiting for us. It'll sure beat the chuck these poor hands have to eat."

They swung along easily. The cows were getting ready to bed down for the night, and some of the hands were already mounted up and riding watch on them, singing their haunting, sad lullabies that warbled on and on like coyote calls. Cookfires were springing up, and over the heavy smell of the tired cattle, the breeze was sweet and cool. Bret pushed his hat back on his head. Pa suddenly reigned in and pointed. "What's going on over there?"

Bret didn't see anything except what he thought was two men dancing a kind of jig by a campfire, but suddenly Pa rode up to them, and they separated. Bret followed and saw that Pa's six-shooter from his waistband was in his hand.

"What're you doing to that boy?" Pa asked. Then Bret saw that a grown man had been hitting a boy of about fifteen or sixteen with a piece of harness strap.

"Who are you to butt in, stranger?" the man asked, furious, keeping a tight hand on the leather strap and taking an angry stride closer to Pa. Pa stayed cool. The hammer of his gun eared back and the muzzle never wavered.

"I'm the law in Waterstop."

"Well I ain't bustin' the law, mister. I'm giving that backward boy there a lesson in plain English. Now you clear out, y'hear?"

"You take one step closer to me or that boy, and I'll give you an answer you won't like," Pa said. "Bret, slide down and get that boy on your horse. He's hurtin', and I won't leave him here."

Bret looked from Pa to the man to the boy, who had fallen to one knee. Then he slid off his horse and approached the boy.

"Where's his folks?" Pa asked.

"Dead. Dead and gone. His cousin's a hand at the ranch I work for, and this boy's our mariann. So you better just—"

"This boy is now a ward of Waterstop, Wyoming, mister. And that's where he's going to stay until I see fit to send him off. You got him, Bret?"

The boy had some difficulty climbing onto the horse's back, but at last Bret got him up, and then he came and swung up behind Pa.

"Can he ride?" Pa asked Bret, without turning his eyes from the angry cowboy. Bret looked back at the boy. "Can you ride?"

But there was no answer. "I reckon he can, Pa," Bret guessed, "if he's worked for a ranch. And he did mount."

Pa let the horse ease back, and Bret's horse followed, eager to get home to its stall. Pa kept the gun up. "Reckon you'll need a new cook's boy. One that ain't so easy to pick on."

Then he urged on the horse, and they rode out of there.

Chapter Eight
The Ward of Waterstop

Doc Chesterton's back office smelled like new paint and fresh paper. He had rows of glass bottles with medicines or cotton wadding in them, clean cloths folded up inside paper wrappers, and charts pinned to the back of the doors. The boy sat on the table staring at the wall. Pa glanced at Bret.

"Stay here with him and the Doc, son. I'm going to check the street. Shouldn't be long."

"Sure, Pa."

Doc Chesterton finished swabbing his hands around in a basin of soap and water and turned to the boy, who sat up on the table without seeming to notice either of the others. There wasn't a flicker of anything in his face—not fear or anger or anything else.

"Now I'd like to take a look at those cuts that rascal gave you," Doc said easily, and he reached out and tried to loosen the boy's shirt from his back. "Bret boy, bring me some more water."

Doc moistened the shirt and took it away in strips, for it had been cut apart by the harness strap. "Well now," he said, adjusting his spectacles. "Not too bad. Reckon the sheriff interfered in plenty of time. We'll just wash you off and send you—" he glanced blankly at Bret.

"Home with me," Bret said. The boy still showed no reaction to anything, only a look of mild disgust when Doc cleaned the four or five cuts on his back.

"Got a name, son?" Doc asked as he worked.

"Joseph," the boy said.

Bret jumped a little at the boy's voice. It was the first time he had spoken.

"Anything else?" Doc asked.

"Joseph. Joseph is enough."

"Been around Indians some," Doc said. It wasn't a question, and the boy didn't answer, but he looked at Doc with more respect.

"Well," Doc added, peeling Joseph's eyelids back one at a time to look at his eyes. "You been underfed and overworked, I imagine. But you're pretty fit. Sheriff says your folks are dead and you got a cousin on one of the ranges around here."

"My partner is on North Rim."

"Where's that?" But Joseph didn't answer. Doc dampened a wide, flat bandage and added, "You're mighty young to be having a partner out there somewheres."

"His name is Micah."

"Hmmm. Don't know anybody by that name. How 'bout you, Bret?"

"Nope," Bret said. Doc gently plastered the bandage against the boy's back and wrapped it into place. It must have hurt like fire, but the boy appeared not to notice any pain.

"About this cousin—" Doc began.

"My partner is on North Rim."

"A canyon rim?" Doc asked.

"Yes—close by. It is a box canyon, and the house is built on a flat place near the top of a mountain. The canyon is on the other side of the mountain. The cabin faces a good valley—trees below, and streams."

"How far from here?"

The boy dropped his eyes, and Bret saw a look of genuine sorrow and chagrin cross the light features of Joseph's face. "Far. I cannot find the way easily. But he called it North Rim, and the canyon on the other side of the mountain was Spear Canyon. It was deep and narrow and rounded on the sides like a straight branch."

Doc shook his head. "There's hundreds of little box canyons between here and the Territory of New Mexico, so I—"

Joseph sighed and bowed his head, then straightened. "It doesn't matter. My partner would not have stayed after I left. I think he left. To find another place."

Doc didn't answer. He only looked thoughtful. He washed his hands and dried them on a towel. "Well, you're about as patched up as I can make you. You go on with Bret for a bite at the sheriff's place. He means to help you out."

Joseph slid off the table and followed Bret out.

"Thanks, Doc," Bret called as they left, but Joseph had fallen back into his silence.

Long shadows cloaked and shrouded the alleys. Fuller's was dark, and so was the once-empty building that had recently been made the bank. The blacksmith's was dark. Everybody was at supper. The hotel dining room, where there were elegant panes of glass and real chintz curtains on the inside, shed a gentle light on the plank sidewalk. From across the wide main street, a jangle of piano music spilled out of the saloon, and the lights were blazing. Bret wondered if there would be trouble that night. Already there were horses lined up at the rail, and the men would be lined up at the bar inside. There would be gambling, too, Pa had said, and fellows losing their pokes pretty quickly and riding out broke.

He shook his head. Didn't make sense to work for months on end and then lose it all in one night. And it didn't make much sense to hire a man to protect the town and yet leave up a building that would make more trouble for everybody. But that was the way it was.

He wasn't thinking much of Joseph right then, and when his companion spoke, Bret jumped a little.

"You're afraid of the saloon?"

"I ain't afraid of anything," Bret said sharply, but Joseph looked him straight in the eye, and so Bret went on, more coolly, "I just wish I could work with Pa tonight, instead of sitting home and waiting like I got to do when there's trouble."

"Micah says the saloons are bad medicine."

"Well, what's that mean?"

"Bad."

"Bad medicine, huh? Guess they are, then. Pa used to make that stuff—whiskey, you know. Then he gave it up and we came out here. And the folks made him sheriff."

"I've seen men with whiskey. I never saw one turn his face away from it." Almost as an afterthought, Joseph added something that was too low to catch.

"What was that?" Bret asked.

"It is the only way I can say it." And he repeated it. But it wasn't intelligible. Indian language.

For a moment Bret said nothing. Few men turned from whiskey, the selling of it or the drinking of it, yet Pa had turned. And all that Pa had been, all the harshness and quick anger, faded more and more the further he got from that business. But somehow it just didn't seem settled for Bret. If only he dared talk things over with Pa, just one time. Not to accuse—but to ask him about the past, about the times he'd gotten so angry with Bret. But just thinking about bringing up the past made Bret feel uneasy. As he and Joseph walked along in silence toward the light thrown out of the saloon doors, Bret noticed that Barton had come out, probably to stroll to the hotel for a little dinner and peace and quiet. The big bartender glanced sharply at them as he stepped into the street, and his eyes fell on Joseph. Suddenly the saloonkeeper turned back and went inside again.

"What was that all about?" Bret mumbled.

Instead of paying attention to the question, Joseph said, "Why did your father stop making the whiskey?"

Bret shrugged off the thought of Barton, and then he replied, "Pa changed after he heard the gospel. He—"

"The black book? The leather book?" Joseph asked suddenly.

"Huh? Yeah, the Bible. Is that what you mean?"

"Yes! Your father heard the words and was converted?"

"Yeah. That's what I was trying to tell you."

Joseph had stopped, and his pale blue eyes looked up, excited, almost frantic. "Then he knows Micah! He must know Micah!"

"Wh-why?"

"Micah said that they were brothers. Any man that kept the words of the leather book was brother to the rest!"

"You don't understand—they're brothers, but they never met. Pa don't know him."

"I will ask him!" Joseph insisted and nodded for Bret to keep walking. "He might know him. He might know the Preacher."

Bret fell silent for a moment, and then he asked at last, "Were you really a friend to some Indians? I never saw any except at a distance."

"Your father turned from whiskey after he read the Bible?" Joseph asked.

"Yes."

Then Joseph was silent again, and Bret could get no answers to anything he said until he had opened the latchstring at the back door of the house and entered with the shirtless orphan boy. And something in the boy's manner kept him from asking if he had even noticed Barton. Perhaps Joseph, head down and mindful of his own pain, hadn't seen Barton on the sidewalk, but Bret felt sure that the two knew each other somehow.

Chapter Nine
Breaking the Colt

Pale shafts of sunlight streamed across the quilt on the bed, falling across it in blocks. On the floor and wrapped in a blanket, Bret rolled over to see if Joseph was awake yet. Pa must have come in after midnight; and judging by the light, he was probably gone already. Joseph had gotten a little feverish the night before, so Bret had left the bed to him and had piled up a makeshift bed on the floor for himself.

"Reckon it's time to get up," Bret ventured. Joseph's only answer was to sit up and kick back the covers. They got into their clothes, and Bret lent the blond-haired boy a shirt to wear.

Joseph seemed to feel better, and his fever was broken. But at the breakfast table he eyed Ma a little distrustfully and didn't have much to say. Ma didn't seem to notice it much.

Certainly the last month had seen many improvements in the kitchen. There were new plates, forks, knives and spoons all around, and cups and saucers for coffee.

Ma dished up hashed potatoes and salt pork for the boys.

"This pork beats beef out an' out, Ma," Bret said, digging into the meat eagerly. "A body sure can get tired of it."

"Barton was knocking, waking Pa up early this morning," Ma said. "He's heard something about trouble for the new bank, and he wants to be deputized again."

At Barton's name, Joseph's keen pale eyes met Ma's. Just as quickly he looked back at his food.

"Pa want me today?" Bret asked eagerly.

"He said something about the men at the livery stable needing a hand with the extra horses. Buyers are coming into town already."

Bret barely held in a sigh of frustration. Watering horses! It was good to work for pay, but he'd rather be helping Pa for free.

Ma smiled a little at him and reached across the table to fill Joseph's cup with coffee. "Are you feeling better today?" she asked.

He looked at her, a little confused, and then finally stammered, "Yes," and gave his head a little jerk for a nod.

"Can you work with horses?" she asked him.

He nodded.

"Well, then, you can both work over there until dinner, I reckon. There's talk of a horse auction in the afternoon if enough of the cattle buyers are interested, and you boys'll be wantin' to see that, so do a good job this morning and Pa and I will let you go."

"Yes, Ma," Bret said, pouring maple syrup over his hash.

"The sheriff will be there?" Joseph asked.

"Yes—Pa. He'll surely stop by," Ma said. "His horse is on loan until he gets a better one for riding the range."

"He has the Bible? Micah had a Bible, too," Joseph said. "He is my partner." He gestured toward the south window. "South of here—several days ride."

He was looking at Ma with a new expression—almost a hopeful one, expecting her to respond.

"Do you know the way?" Ma asked.

Joseph looked discouraged and shot a glance of understanding at Bret, as though acknowledging that Bret had been correct in saying his parents wouldn't know Micah. "I might find the way," he faltered. "It was not so long ago that I came this way. I must earn the money to go and find him."

"Well—" and Ma's voice softened—"I reckon you'll be glad of some extra work at the livery, then, and if we start to having public horse auctions, we can maybe find a good bargain on a horse for you."

Joseph said no more, but through the rest of the meal Bret saw a change in him. He adopted a gentleness with Ma and answered her more than he had answered Bret.

"Was your friend Micah a prospector?" Ma asked him.

"He panned for gold," Joseph said.

"Had a Bible, did he?"

"Yes. A leather book that he said had God's words in it."

"Do you reckon he was right about that?"

For a moment Joseph's face went back to its stoic expression, and Bret thought he might not answer, but then he admitted, "Perhaps. Micah spoke many things strange to hear from his book. The heart could not hold it all at once. He told me that."

Then he said no more, and they finished quickly. He stacked the dishes neatly for Ma to wash, and he and Bret left for the livery stable.

"Your mother will let me keep the money I earn?" he asked Bret when they were out in the wide and dusty street.

"Sure."

Joseph looked thoughtful. "A woman might," he said at last. "But the sheriff? Would he?"

"Of course he would!" Bret exclaimed, half annoyed at the question. "Pa's already took pretty good care of you, ain't he?"

Joseph didn't answer, and Bret regretted the annoyance in his tone. Joseph hadn't been brought up to understand common decency among folks—it wasn't his fault if he couldn't trust them right off.

"But who will board me?" Joseph asked at last.

"Why, we will, of course!"

"For no pay?"

"You'll have to help with chores, I guess, just like me."

"Micah was like this," Joseph said, stopping Bret from entering the front of the livery stable. "He said 'share and share alike,' and he gave me a bag of gold when I left him."

"Where is it now?"

"My cousin took it. He said he would hold it for me, and he gambled it away."

"That was pretty rotten."

"I should have realized it. I should have been careful." Then he shook his head and sighed as though he had a lot to think about, and they went inside.

A cool breeze was drifting through the big stable. The back doors were open to the wide grasslands, and the mountains were a line of blurry blue in the background. The sweet smell of hay mixed with the heavy smell of horses was carried on the breeze.

"Howdy, boys!" Reed Hauser called out. "Bret, you can take a hand at mucking out the stalls, and we'll let your buddy there pitch down a little breakfast fer some of the new arrivals. We got some more out back in the remuda, so light a shuck."

"Sure, Mr. Hauser."

Joseph had already inspected a clutter of tools in one corner and had taken a pitchfork and sickle. He scrambled up the ladder. Bret wondered what he needed a sickle for, but dismissed the question and set to work.

It was nice to be around the gentle, tired workhorses and the beautiful, high-spirited mustangs that rolled their eyes at newcomers and lifted a hoof every now and then as though inviting a fight. Out back were the colts that had never been ridden.

For a couple of hours they mostly worked in silence while Hauser chatted in the wide front doorway with cowboys or buyers or some of the storekeepers. Right at eleven he came back to the stalls and called out, "Come on boys, let's tire them colts out a little before the auction."

Bret eagerly laid his pitchfork aside. He'd never busted a bronco before, but he'd seen some of the cowboys taking the kinks out of their half-wild remuda horses, and he wanted to try.

Reed Hauser seemed to understand.

"Wanna take a try?" he asked Bret. Some other men were gathered around the remuda and were leaning on the poles of the fence. They were horse owners and buyers, and they all knew horses pretty well.

"Sure," Bret said. "I ain't never done it before, but I'll take a turn on it."

Some of the men hooted and called out, "Sure, let him try, Reed!"

Mr. Hauser grinned. "Well, pick him out a gentle one, boys, and we'll see how he does."

The big remuda was fenced in with freshly cut poles, but there was a section off to one side with a gate so that a horse could be separated and trotted around without everyone pawing him and making him shy.

One of the men uncoiled his lariat and with an almost careless gesture snapped a loop out and dropped it over the head of a chestnut colt that snorted and drew back from the line.

"Easy now, easy," he called, working up the line, hand over hand. The other horses retreated, and the man finally calmed the colt and stood talking to it.

"May as well saddle it up," Hauser observed carelessly. "Give him a good chance. There's a breakin' saddle on the rail just inside the door."

Pretty soon the chestnut was saddled up and waiting in the tiny corral. Bret climbed up on the fence and dropped inside. The man holding the horse said, "Now just relax everything that you can relax, and keep your leg muscles tight. Time his head when he dips it, or he'll fling you forward."

"Okay." Bret saw that Joseph was watching intently. He got his foot in the stirrup and swung up, grabbed the reins in one hand like he'd seen the cowpokes do, and nodded to the man. "Let 'er go."

For a moment the horse just stood there. Then Bret saw Joseph and the men whiz by in a circle, and it made his head spin to see them go like that. There was a terrific thump, a pain that sprouted between his shoulder blades, and he instantly knew what the expression "to have your ears ring" meant. It was a hollow ring, not a high one like a bell. Gasping, he tried to sit up. The horse, tossing its head and shaking its mane, trotted to the other side of the corral.

Some of the men slapped their thighs and laughed. Bret shook his head and managed to stand up.

"Let him try again!" one of them called.

"Sure, if he's willing!" someone added.

His teeth ached from hitting each other, but Bret pinched his lips together the way Pa did when he was all-fired determined, and he said, "I reckon I'll try again."

"Thatta' boy! Ain't no horse yet that couldn't be rode by a man with gumption," one of the men added.

Hauser himself brought the horse back. It eyed Bret and shook its mane, ready for another contest. Bret swung up, and Hauser let go.

This time the horse took off right away, one buck and then a series of little crowhops that Bret discovered he could handle as long as he timed them right. But then the same thing happened—everything turned in a circle, and next thing he knew he was on the ground, half senseless.

"You got to watch his head, boy, not the countryside," somebody was saying—somebody with a red flannel shirt and strong wiry arms that pulled him to his feet. That was the only thing Bret could focus on for a moment.

"One more time," Bret said. It was like Pa said. A man in the West had to be ready to prove himself or he'd never have peace.

"No, Bret. Too much learnin' ain't good for a feller," Hauser said kindly. "You can try again next time. How about your pardner over there? What's his name?"

"Joseph."

"How about it, Joseph? Wanna try?" Hauser asked.

Joseph swung over the fence and waited while Hauser brought the horse back. Bret saw that he'd thrust the sickle into his belt. But Joseph paused to drop it outside the ring. He took the horse's bridle himself, and gestured for Hauser to move aside. Then he petted the horse's nose and cheek, patted its sleek neck, and gradually worked his way back to the saddle, holding the reins loosely in one hand and talking to the horse the whole time. He slid his hand along the strong ripply shoulder and then gracefully swung up. Instantly the horse broke into an anxious trot and crowhopped around the corral. But he didn't buck much. After a few minutes he came around the corral once in a trot, and then Joseph slid off, rubbed the animal's shoulder, and walked back across the corral.

"Now where'd he learn to do that?" Hauser asked.

Joseph had heard the man as he stopped to retrieve his sickle, but he made no answer, only shoving the sickle back down into his belt.

Chapter Ten
Confrontation

The streets pretty much cleared up during dinner. Reed Hauser offered to take the two boys over to the hotel for their midday meal.

"Just said hello to your Pa and told him I'd take you over for a bite," he told Bret. "Reckon you boys both earned it."

"Sure, thanks, Mr. Hauser."

"You gonna leave that doodad in your belt, boy?" Hauser asked Joseph, nodding at the sickle, but Joseph didn't answer.

Hauser shrugged, and they crossed the street. Coming up from the livery stable, some of the men were wandering into the saloon. Pa was nowhere in sight.

The hotel dining room was crowded. Hauser found them a place at one of the long tables where most of the cowpokes were pushed together. There was stew on the table in big bowls, some beef for slicing, cornbread, beans, and coffee. One of the hotel girls came out every now and then with a fresh bowl and took away an empty one. The room was cluttered with talk and elbows, wool shirts, and big boots thrust out from under the tables.

Bret saw that Joseph cast a wary eye over everything, and the boy that had not feared to mount a wild colt hung back a moment behind Hauser when they entered the crowded room.

Then Bret remembered the confrontation out at the camps. And word had it that Joseph had a cousin at one of the ranches. Could be the boy feared being taken back.

"Say Joe," Bret whispered while Mr. Hauser reached for the big bowl of stew, "if there's trouble with anyone from your old outfit, I'll give you a hand, and so will Hauser."

Joseph answered nothing, only looked back at him, but suddenly Bret read the other boy's steady eye, and he felt sure that suddenly they were friends and that Joseph was glad of the offer for help.

Then they fell to eating. After they were done the girl brought each of them a big piece of dried apple pie drenched with cream. Some of the men leaned back, satisfied. Most of them began to pick up and leave, wanting to get a good place at the horse auction. A couple lingered to talk and speculate on what the animals would bring.

Hauser threw down his napkin. "Might as well get the ball rollin' over there," he said. "You boys can still help if you want—lead 'em out and keep 'em watered for me."

"Sure," Bret said.

They stood up from the bench, and Hauser flipped six bits onto the slightly soiled white cloth before stumping out.

A crowd was gathering around the livery stable. Up the street, men were coming from the saloon and from the checker game at Fuller's. "Looks like the grocery and saloon are gonna close for the event," Bret observed. Joseph's hand dropped to his belt as he watched.

"Where is the saloonkeeper?" he asked.

"I dunno. He's probably at the remuda already. One of his helpers can close up for him, I guess."

"There he is!" Joseph exclaimed, pointing to the big beefy saloonkeeper, who was trying to push his way among the crowd of men at the entrance of the stable.

"Barton!" Joseph cried, and Bret saw that the sickle was clutched in his hand. With a blur of his hand, Joseph brought the sickle back and threw it with a twisting curve, right at Barton. "Barton!" he yelled again.

What saved Barton was turning at the sound of his name. The sickle sank point first into the front of the livery stable. The men up front in the crowd were pushing and calling to each other, but the men in the back fell silent and watched.

"Joseph!" Bret cried. But the other boy strode across the street toward Barton. Every line of him was taut and ready to fight and angry that the sickle had missed.

"I meant to kill you!" he cried. "And I will!"

Barton ignored the weapon embedded in the wall and turned to face him. "You backward stripling. You'll wish that had killed me."

"I already do."

Joseph kept coming, and Bret jumped after him. "Joe, don't! You can't! Stop!"

"Stay out of this, sheriff's kid!" Barton ordered. "Your pappy ain't here to stop me from giving this mute moron what he deserves once't and for all." And he suddenly lunged at Joseph, who by now was only two feet away, and knocked him clean over with a punch to the jaw.

The blond boy hit the ground as hard as Bret had hit it when the horse had bucked him. Barton leaned forward and grabbed the senseless boy's shirt, pulled him up, and hit him again.

"Don't!" Bret cried, and rammed into Barton with his shoulder. Something remorseless like machinery grabbed his hair and threw him back, and he knew that Barton was going to hit him, too, when suddenly there was a horse snorting right over him, and he rolled over Joseph to protect the unconscious boy from being trampled. For an instant he thought his life was over, but then he heard voices and looked up. The horse was between him and Barton. A man in black sat astride the horse, looking down at Barton on the other side. Bret had only met him once before, at a church service held just after they had moved into Waterstop.

"Preacher!" Bret exclaimed in relief. He struggled to a sitting position and watched Barton go back to the livery stable. The saloonkeeper took the sickle out of the wall and strode back toward the Preacher.

"Back off, sky-pilot. Them boys started this, and I aim to finish it," Barton said.

The Preacher had a rifle and sheath on his saddle, but he didn't reach for it.

"Sorry. Bret was just helping out. But I know the blond boy, and I'm putting him under my care. Why was he so angry with you?"

"You're so all-fired set on heaven, mister—I'll be glad to send you there—"

"Put it down, Barton." It was Doc Chesterton, and he had a rifle in his hands. "There's law in Waterstop, and I reckon we'll let Sheriff deal with Joseph about throwin' that sickle at you."

Some of the men standing around didn't look very pleased at the Doc's words. They thought Joseph deserved a beating for what he had done. Bret turned to look at the blond boy, who had been sprawled out alongside him in the dust. Joseph stirred and lifted his head, put a hand to his chin. "Where has he gone?"

"He's on the other side of the horse, but you stay put!" Bret said irritably.

"Why did he not kill me?" Joseph raised himself on his elbows.

"Because no one would let him, that's why!"

"He was at the camp!" Joseph exclaimed. "Ask him yourself! I know Barton! Ask him why I will kill him! He took my money from my cousin! And he beat me when I tried to get it back!"

"That so, Barton?" Doc asked.

"That boy's fool cousin gambled some gold away and the boy got mad and—" Barton threw down the sickle as though disgusted, but Bret saw that he was white under his tan, humiliated at the accusation in front of half the men of the town, who were eagerly looking on. "That boy's backward, as anyone can see what's got eyes in his head. You better tell your Pa to keep him away from me, Jensen kid," Barton said, and stamped back up to the saloon.

Bret helped Joseph up, and then Joseph looked up and saw the Preacher for the first time.

"Preacher!" he cried, and grabbed the man's boot, leaning against the horse. The tall, slim man smiled at him.

"You are a fair piece away from Micah," he said. "I heard about your cousin taking you away. I guess it didn't work out."

"He took my money, and then Barton came out to the ranch house and made him drunk and gambled it away from him!" Joseph's eyes turned from anger to pleading. "Can you take me to Micah?"

"I don't know where he is, son. He's left the cabin."

Chapter Eleven
Doc's Offer

Pa looked mighty mad when Bret told him about the fight in the street. In fact, Bret hadn't seen Pa look that way since before the camp meeting where he'd gotten saved.

"Threw you by your hair, huh? That sounds like Barton, all right. Mean as a rattlesnake with a dent in its tail."

"Now Felix," Ma told him gently. "What could he think when Joseph threw a sickle at him?"

"Or did he just recognize Joseph and decide to shut him up?" Pa asked. "Joseph's cousin lost that money to Barton—and no doubt they played their hands when Barton had him half-full of that there whiskey he makes!"

"At least Barton can't keep insisting on an election and putting himself up for sheriff against you," Ma told him. "The Lord took care of that by disgracing Barton, but—" And her eyes glanced over at Joseph, who stood by the sitting-room stove with his head down in defiance.

Bret shifted uncomfortably. The anger in Pa's eyes drained away at the slim blond boy, who stood rigid and rebellious across the room from him.

"Joseph," Pa said, his voice heavy and serious, "if you had killed Barton, you'd likely be hung by now. Mobs don't bother to consider a boy's age."

"I'm not afraid to die!" he returned hotly.

"But I'd hate to see you get killed," Pa told him. "You got off a mite easy this time. Barton's too embarrassed to make a big to-do about what you did, but I can't let such a thing go on from a boy that's under my own roof."

"Turn me away, I don't care! Barton's a thief, and I want to kill him!"

"Still?" Pa asked. "Even after you almost got Bret killed, too?"

Joseph was silent and sullen.

"I figure folks have treated you right badly, Joseph. More like you were a slave than a young man, but in this house you're going to be treated like a young man, like my own son."

At this Joseph lifted a cautious eye to Pa.

"Every man that's free-born takes his punishment like a man," Pa said. "And that punishment don't come like stripes laid across your back from a harness strap. I don't mean to hurt you like that by whipping you like a dog. But I do mean to give you a switching out back, and I mean you to come out and take it like a man and like a son of mine."

Joseph lifted his eyes to Pa, and for a moment they looked at each other across the room. Bret's stomach knotted up. Pa hadn't licked him since—well, since before Pa'd converted. Maybe it would be different, now.

Joseph's eyes were big, even though he tried to look brave. Bret saw that Pa's verdict had torn him with fear.

"Now I'm goin' out to get a switch from the woodpile, and I expect you to be there in a minute or so." And he tramped out across the room, into the kitchen. They heard the back door swing shut behind him.

Joseph looked at Bret, and Bret looked down. Pa didn't sound angry, just firm. Maybe it wouldn't be so bad.

Head down, Joseph walked across the room and into the kitchen. In another moment Bret heard the back door swing shut again. He looked at Ma.

"Pa used to hurt me a lot when he whipped me," he ventured.

"Pa's a different man now," Ma told him. "Couldn't you see that?"

And then Bret could see it—the firmness, the promise not to be cruel, the explanation to Joseph. All of those were new. Bret tried to relax at the thought that Pa's change was real.

They waited in the front room for several minutes.

"Well, he must be finished by now," Ma said. "I've got to tend to supper. Come and set the table, son."

He followed her into the kitchen and set out the plates, forks, knives, and spoons. Still, nobody came in. He set out the cups and saucers and nobody came. At last he peeked out the back door. He got just a glimpse of Pa and Joseph together, Pa holding the blond boy by the shoulders, and Joseph crying. A sturdy switch lay on the ground. But it was Pa's face, the kindness on it, that surprised Bret. And to think he was comforting the boy after giving him a hiding with a switch.

He never did that for me, Bret thought, and closed the door softly.

After a while, Pa and Joseph came in while Ma and Bret studiously tended to the meal at the stove. But Bret stole a glance at them, at Pa's arm around the boy's shoulders.

"Now we'll forget about it," Pa said. "Over and done with, and I'm right glad to have you in my home. Go and wash your face."

Bret turned back to the coffeepot, but his face burned. He didn't know why.

Dinner was quiet, and Joseph took his chair gingerly enough. Pa had been careful not to hit his injured back, but it was apparent that every time Joseph sat down that night, he'd have some thinking to do.

After dinner they took their coffee into the parlor. Once again the conversation turned to Barton.

"A mayor could make him shut that saloon down, at least on Sundays," Ma protested. "I wish he would realize the misery he causes and just leave town once and for all!"

Pa threw his free hand into the air and sank into a chair. "Who am I kiddin', Nance? I was Barton myself a year and a half ago." He sighed. "I wonder how many kids are wastin' away in Tennessee and North Carolina wishin' they had a shot at me for what I did?"

"No use in goin' on about what God's forgiven, Felix."

"Isn't there? I'm forgiven, but there's still men I turned into paupers with moonshine." Pa stood up and walked restlessly to the front window. He pushed aside the chintz curtains and stared out into the street.

"You have to realize that the good Lord has His control over them just like He has on you," Ma said. "A man, no matter how wicked, wasn't ever so powerful that he thwarted God."

Pa looked at her and then sighed. "Guess you're right. But sometimes I sure wish I could do it over again. Anyway, it isn't right to feel smug around Barton because he's a saloonkeeper. Smugness never turned a man to God; compassion did."

"How is this that your God does such things?" Joseph asked suddenly. "Were you like him?" By "him" he meant Barton.

"Yes," Pa said, looking at Joseph, who was hunkered down by the parlor stove. "Worse, I think, because of the way I used to treat my wife and Bret." At Pa's words, Bret's face flamed up again, but nobody noticed.

"And all this comes from that book?" Joseph asked.

"The Bible. Yes."

"Then why not read to him from the book?"

"I would, if he'd listen, Joseph. And Preacher's come to try, that's for sure. Guess he heard about all the cowboys comin' in, and he wants to have some extra meetings." The pensive expression left Pa's face as he thought of something new. "But see here, boy, I'll look into what Barton did, and if he got your cousin drunk to bilk him of that gold, well, he'll pay for it."

Suddenly there was a knock on the door. Pa went and answered. "Doc! Come in!" And he stepped aside for Doc Chesterton.

"Hello, Felix. How do, Mrs. Jensen? Bret? Joseph?"

"Trouble, Doc?" Pa asked. "Or is this a visit?"

"A visit."

"Well, sit down."

"It's kind of business, too," Doc admitted, sitting down in the rocking chair while Pa settled down on the sofa next to Ma.

"I've been needing an assistant at the apothecary, and Reed tells me that Joseph here wants steady work. Will you let him work for me?"

"That's mighty nice of you, Doc," Pa said. "Course, the boy's been alone quite a bit and was enjoying himself with Bret, there."

"Well, boys'll be boys," Doc agreed. "From what I saw this afternoon, they were enjoyin' themselves plenty."

Both Bret and Joseph looked down at that, but Doc went on. "Well, I need a boy that's got some hard sand in his craw. I figure Joseph's got it, and he wants to earn some money—I even heard they was bustin' a bronc earlier—"

"They what?" Ma gasped.

"Maybe Doc would like some tea, Ma; should I get it?" Bret asked.

"I reckon I can fix the Doc's tea, Bret Matthew," Ma said. Joseph gave Bret a dig in the ribs and grinned.

Pa glanced at Joseph. "Well, Joseph? I'll leave it up to you. I know you want to save up and move out."

For a moment Joseph looked blank at the suggestion, and then he said, "I would like a steady job so that I could save my money."

"You able to work with a sawbones?"

"Yes, I can."

"Well, that's settled," Doc said, stretching his legs so that his well-polished boots showed up to the ankles. "Eight o'clock in the morning. I'll see you then."

Joseph's silence was his assent. Bret sighed, a little regretfully. Joseph could annoy him by getting into fights with big men like Bill Barton, but at the same time it was interesting to be around him, and friends were scarce out here, just like they'd been scarce when Pa had been moonshining.

It wasn't until that evening, when they were pulling off their boots for bed, that Joseph said anything along the same line.

Ma had fixed up a cot, and the two had agreed to trade off for it. Joseph stood by the high bed, and Bret sat with his back to the blond boy while he struggled to get his boots off.

"I did not feel Barton's second punch," Joseph said, and Bret turned around, surprised to hear the other boy talk first.

"No, I guess he put your lights out with the first one," he agreed. "I shoulder-charged him when I saw he meant to keep hitting."

"Good friend," Joseph said at last. "To fight with me against Barton."

"You were in trouble."

"I lived with the Indians, you know; every stranger is an enemy. Even the words are one word in their language—in the language of the Arapaho."

"Was that where that fellow Micah made friends with you?"

"No. I was given to white men as trade for guns and whiskey, and they gave me to men to work for them on a cattle drive. The cook was good to me, but the other men were cruel sometimes because I was a boy. Then I worked at a ranch, but I ran away on another drive when I saw smoke in the hills, and I found Micah, and he made me his partner."

"That was right nice of him."

Joseph fiddled with the buttons on his shirt. "He was the first person to be kind to me—like a friend. And he read a Bible. And now your father—he says he will let me save my money."

"Sure. Pa will. He knows you want to find Micah again." Bret paused, and then spoke again. "Say, Joseph, can I ask you something?"

"What?"

"What do you believe about God?"

Joseph shrugged and kept his eyes down. "So many of the white men—they called the Indians heathen. The whites called themselves Christians. Then Micah told me that not every man who calls himself a Christian really is one—that only men who really believed the special Book were true Christians. Yet the Indians, they know nothing about Christians or Bibles. They taught me about the spirits that move through the heavens and the earth. It is hard to know. Tomorrow I will find the Preacher and ask him how best to find Micah again. Perhaps soon I will rejoin him. He could answer my questions."

Chapter Twelve
A Spell of Trouble

"School'll be starting in less than a month. I declare, Bret, these vittles has made you shoot up again!" Ma exclaimed. "Your wrists are straining right out of those cuffs! You'd best go put on one of Pa's workshirts, or you'll be ripping the elbows out of this one."

"Sure, Ma. Say, you ain't going to make me go to school again, are you?"

"I'm going over to Fuller's to find some material for that very thing. You'll need some new clothes, and I have time to sew them for you. What's more, there's a seamstress at the dry goods store, and for two bits she'll sew you up a shirt. I think I'll ask Pa if we can afford to have her make you two."

"Oh, Ma! I'm almost sixteen. I can read and cipher all right—"

"Not another word. I won't have you standing about idle all day. And I won't have you spending the rest of your days as a hired hand in a livery stable."

"It ain't the livery stable, Ma. I don't care so much about that, but—now that I'm almost sixteen—do you think that maybe, maybe—"

He had her curiosity up now. Bret wondered how she could not have noticed how much he wanted to be a lawman someday.

"Maybe what, son?"

"Maybe I could be Pa's deputy?"

It was the first time Bret ever saw a woman go so white as to faint. In another instant he had a chair under her. He stood over her and fanned her with his hat.

"Ma! Ma, what's the matter?"

"Bret boy, don't tell me you're serious. Oh, I can see it in your eyes that you are—and you such a good boy, too!"

"But Ma, the town needs—"

"Don't, boy, don't ever say it unless you're willing to see your Ma pass on to glory. I just couldn't take it if both of you was lawmen."

"S-sure Ma, sure." He glumly plopped his hat back on his head and stood over her uncertainly while she panted and fanned herself with her limp hand.

"I reckon I'll see if Joseph's ready for supper soon. You all right?" Bret asked miserably.

"Fine, fine. Only please don't ever scare me so much again, son."

Bret clumped out of the house, hand in his back pocket, head slouched between his shoulders. The street was quiet, but he could hear the whooping of the cowboys as they herded their cows toward the chutes for loading up. Waterstop was going to be one rich town before long, once all the cattle were paid for.

Joseph was out in front of Doc's, sweeping the plank sidewalk that had recently been put in. He looked up as Bret approached, and though his lips didn't smile, his eyes welcomed the other boy.

"Have you seen Preacher?" the blond boy asked.

"No. I'd figgered he'd be out about the town," Bret said. "Thought you'd have seen him long before I did."

"He has not come looking for me," Joseph said, looking down as he worked on the sidewalk. "If anybody could lead me to Micah, he could. And I thought he surely would, for he is a man of the Bible, like Micah. Perhaps I must work a while. Perhaps he wished me to earn my way."

"Well, seems like he'd surely talk to you about it."

Just then a shot rang out from across the street. The two boys glanced at each other. Joseph laid the broom against a post.

"Sounds like it's comin' from the bar," Bret guessed.

"It is early yet." Joseph glanced up at the sky. "Yet some of the men have been paid. I saw my cousin go into the saloon a few minutes ago."

"Hope they ain't fightin' in there—" Bret didn't bother finishing. More shots rang out, and suddenly two men crashed through the swinging doors and landed in the street. Already somebody bawled out, "Sheriff, get the sheriff!" And people came running from the stores and their work to see what was going on. Doc Chesterton came out of his office and looked at the boys in turn. "Guess we better get the operatin' table ready, Joseph."

The blond boy nodded and turned to go in, and then stopped and pointed. "There is the sheriff."

Sure enough, it was Pa. He raced through the people and was soon hidden by the small crowd.

"Oh, he'll break it up," Doc said lazily. "Too early yet for a real whizz-banger."

There were more shots that suddenly barked from the crowd, and a woman screamed. Men yelled. Doc stopped and so did Joseph.

"Get me my bag!" Doc called as he bounded into the street, and then someone cried, "The sheriff! He's shot the sheriff!"

Chapter Thirteen
Facing Down the Mob

The street was lit up in bright splotches with the glare of torches. There was one man at one end of town, and there was another at the other end. And each had a group clustered around him. Over the hot and still night air, Bret heard their voices, more high-pitched and angry than a man's ought to be. He kept his arms around Ma, but deep down inside him there was fear gnawing his vitals.

"Are you praying, son? Are you praying like we did the first night Pa went out?"

"Sure, Ma—but it's distracting me. Those men—"

But Ma seemed unconscious of them. "Surely the good Lord wouldn't take Pa from us, Bret. Not now—not when it seems like we just got him back."

Her words recalled him to his own troubles, to their troubles. Doc was still in the back office, with Pa stretched out on the table and Joseph standing by to help. The bullet had gone into Pa's side pretty deep.

Out on the street, which Bret could see through the wide windows of the front office, there were shouts from the various knots of people. Others were drifting onto the street from the hotel or saloon or even from some of the houses back of town. Two men suddenly thundered up the street past the jail house. They were mounted on black horses, and they dragged a stuffed scarecrow behind the horses.

"You're trembling, son."

"Didn't you see the street, Ma? Something awful's about to bust loose."

"No. What?" She looked up at him. "I heard horses ride by."

"They're fixing to lynch that fellow that shot Pa. There's two mobs a-gathering."

Ma turned and looked, for the first time realizing what the groups and the haranguing speeches added up to.

Through the flickering and dancing shadows on the street, a tall black shadow moved with certainty, striding toward the doc's office. It relentlessly pushed past the smaller knots of men, a huge clipper ship undaunted by smaller vessels out there in the sea of black night and torch flame.

"It's Barton!" Bret whispered, and tightened his hold on Ma. Figure it to be Barton, now with Pa down wounded and a score to settle with Bret and Joseph, he told himself. There was no time to get Ma away from there, not without taking her out into the wild street where Barton would see them and perhaps follow.

Ma was scared, too. They both watched in silence as the enormous figure came all the way across the street, up onto the sidewalk with two stamps of the big boots, and into the front door. For a moment Barton stood framed in the doorway, his head almost touching the lintel.

"Well?" he growled. "Will he live?"

Neither mother nor son said anything.

"I don't aim to hurt you, boy. Speak up. Will he live? There's murder fixin' to be done tonight, and your Pa's the only one that can stop it."

"Doc's still with him," Bret said in a low voice.

"He was a fool to walk into a drunk like that, one that had a gun in his hand. That cowpoke couldn't tell a sheriff from the president. That's why he shot him."

Despite his fear, Bret felt his cheeks tingle with warmth. Pa was no fool. And if men like Barton didn't sell the stuff to armed men—

"How'd he get the gun, anyway?" Bret returned. "You gave your word that the men in the saloon would check their guns."

"I can't see everything. And that poor dumb cowboy ain't got a murderin' bone in his body," Barton returned. "Those folks plan to lynch him for a-killin' the sheriff. And that poor kid's scared sober. He didn't know what he was doin'. He'll never touch liquor again, and I'll be the first to tell your Pa that if he lives. Come on, Doc!" he suddenly bawled. "There's a crowd outside! We need the sheriff!"

The door to the inner office suddenly swung open, as if in answer. Framed in the lamplight from the operating room, Doc Chesterton looked at Barton. "What's the problem here?" Then he looked past Barton to the street. "Hmph. 'Fraid of that. That boy safe in jail?"

"Not for long. They'll tear it down."

Sweat streamed down Doc's wrinkled and saggy face. The front of his white shirt was spattered from doing the surgery. Joseph stood by the table, face impassive as always, but his eyes looked right at Bret's. Yet Bret could not read the expression.

Pa lay on the table, a sheet pulled up over his chest. Yet there were bandages, too, plainly visible on the left side and wound around him. His eyes fluttered open and he looked first at Ma. Then he smiled a little.

"Jensen," Barton said. "The town's fixin' to lynch that kid. You got to save him."

Puzzlement flicked across Pa's weary eyes. "How?" he whispered.

"You got to go out there tonight like you ain't even scratched, and tell those folks to go home."

"Are you mad?" Ma asked. "He can't do that. He's been shot!"

Pa lay silent and looked at Barton. For a moment nobody in the room made a sound. At last Barton said, "I hear them out there, Jensen. Can't you hear them gettin' ready?"

"I hear them," Pa whispered.

"Ain't no love lost betwixt you and me, but I don't hanker to stand by and see this."

No, Bret thought savagely, not with all the trouble having come from your liquor. But he said nothing. Only his insides burned with anger.

"Preacher can't help?" Pa gasped.

"Preacher's gone. Left late last night," Barton said.

Joseph looked up, startled, and a puzzled wrinkle crossed Pa's forehead. But the expression passed, and he was silent a moment. When he spoke, his voice was calmer and stronger; "If you can help me across the street, I can speak to them, I think."

"I'll get you over there. It'll only have to last for a minute—what you say. And I'll back you up. They won't turn against you—not with feeling for you running so high," Barton said.

"Felix—" Ma began. But Pa forced himself to raise his hand. "I got to. No lynchings here—now or ever. Help me up, somebody. Get me a shirt."

"Might just start to bleed again," Doc put in. "Might not. It's up to you."

"Can't let them hurt that kid. A shirt."

"Your boots first," Joseph said, and knelt to push the boots up on Pa's feet. Pa leaned against Doc, but there was a little bit of color in his cheeks. He was determined to fight it out against the pain and weakness.

Doc sent Bret to fetch a shirt of the Doc's, and Barton and Ma managed to get it up Pa's arms, though when Pa moved the left arm he groaned some.

They got him on his feet, supported between Bret and Barton. Pa couldn't hold his head up a minute. Bret could see him fighting down the pain. At last he nodded, though the sweat streamed off his face.

"Everybody here—deputized," he said at last. "Joseph, you take the gun from my holster. Bret—my waistband gun's on the table yonder. Doc, grab one of your own and come on."

Ma said nothing as they went out through the front office and into the hot night. Both the mobs had come together near the jailhouse, and men were calling out to the wretched prisoner inside.

"Get us through the crowd," Pa said to Barton, and he put as much authority into his voice as he could.

"It's the sheriff—Sheriff's got something to say," Barton growled as his bulk plowed a way through the sea of people.

Someone had been standing on a wooden crate up by the jail to talk. Barton pulled him down with a surly excuse—"Make way for the sheriff—" and he and Bret pushed Pa up onto the box. Pa's knees swayed, but then became still.

"Folks of Waterstop!" he exclaimed. "There hasn't been any murder done! Put down your torches and guns and go home! There ain't gonna be no lynchings in this here town!"

Somebody in the sea of faces shouted something in return, something about a no-good drifter getting his deserts. But already some of the people looked agreeable, even a little startled at seeing Pa before them, not much worse from a bullet.

"Go home!" he called again. "There's been enough shooting done and enough violence! Go home!"

Some of the people even began to drift away on this command.

But others stayed, and some were uncertain. Their bodies were pressed close together in a sweating, steaming huddle around the jail. It was enough to make anybody feel frantic, Bret thought. But he stayed as calm as he could.

"Pull your guns when I signal, but don't fire," Pa ordered his deputies. "Wait for my signal." Then he called, "I got four deputies here with orders to drop any man what forces a way into this jail!" In a lower voice he said, "Show 'em, boys!" And Bret, Joseph, Doc, and Barton drew their guns.

The crowd fell back in a wave.

"Go home!" Pa cried. "Ain't nobody been killed! Go home or run the risk yourself of being arrested or shot up if it comes to a fight. Go home!"

In little groups the crowd dispersed, hurriedly, sneakily, as men came to their senses apart from the mob and scurried away. Pa suddenly toppled from the crate, but Barton caught him, and nobody seemed to notice, now that the crowd had thinned out so much.

"Let's get him home where Nance can take care of him," Doc ordered. He and Barton carried Pa across the street, keeping to the shadows. Bret and Joseph followed along behind.

Chapter Fourteen
Midnight Discussion

Moonlight streamed across the high bed. Bret lay and watched it for a while. At last he sat up, pulled his knees to his chin, and sat with head bowed.

"You are worried for your father, Bret?" Joseph asked.

"I didn't mean to wake you, Joe," Bret said. There was no answer. The boy was waiting for Bret to reply to his question. "I don't reckon I'm worried about Pa dying, Joseph. Doc thinks he'll be okay in a week or so. And I feel it myself that he's gonna get better." He looked down between his knees at the cover. "It's something else."

Then they were both silent, but as Bret's eyes adjusted to the gloom where the cot was, he could see that Joseph had sat up and was waiting, relaxed, for Bret to either speak or to be silent. In either case, Bret realized, Joseph would wait with him. Once a fellow got to understand the blond boy's ways, he could see that Joseph was a good friend.

"You know Pa used to be different, Joseph?"

"Yes, before he became a true Christian."

"I was different back then, too."

At that Joseph was silent, and Bret realized that the other boy would not pry. But at last the boy said, "Was that before you became a Christian?"

"Well, not really. I was a Christian, and I tried to take care of Ma when Pa was gone out with the other men, making moonshine or selling it or fighting or playing cards. But inside, I guess I hated Pa a lot."

Joseph kept his eyes fixed on him through the gloom, and waited for Bret to go on.

"When Pa repented and got saved, I felt like it wasn't real," Bret admitted. "I thought maybe he just felt guilty and had had too much to drink—he was crying so hard over the preacher. I got kind of mad when he put his arms around me."

A lump came up in his throat. Bret swallowed it and went on. "Then we moved out West, and it was so tough—everything went wrong, it seemed. The oxen got sick and died, and then we got horses that were only half broke, and a river rose right before we crossed it and we lost half our stuff—and every time something went wrong, Pa would be standing by, saying we had to pray about it. I got mad at him, I guess. Seemed like he had no right to talk like that after the way he'd been before."

"But he was truly changed," Joseph said.

"Well, I guess after a while of working together with him, I got to like him more and got over being mad. We were on the trail for a long time, and he and Ma and I got to know each other a lot more than I ever thought we could."

Then they were silent again. "Thing is—" Bret faltered. "I—there's a difference between liking your Pa and thinking a lot of him. Between liking him and trusting him. And now I just get the idea that Pa's the best Pa in the whole country. I get the idea that I couldn't have anybody better. You saw him tonight, Joseph. There ain't a braver or calmer man anywhere around."

"Then you're happy," Joseph said.

"Yeah, sure. I am. But at the same time, I feel like—well, like I've done something wrong, too. I didn't trust him. I kept waitin' for him to go back to what he was before. And then when I saw him bein' kind to you, I got a little jealous—not that I didn't want him to be kind to you—I did. But I wanted him to be kind to me, too, only I was too proud to ask him. Now I feel like I don't deserve him. I know what made him such a good man—it was the Lord."

"You think so?" Bret didn't catch the sudden intensity in Joseph's voice.

"And I don't think I love the Lord like Pa does. I don't think I'd have enough faith and guts to get up after I been shot and face a mob. Maybe that's what God's trying to tell me tonight—I'm just not all the man I thought I was."

"You think God Himself is keeping you awake to speak to you?"

"Sure. I've been lying here wrestling with something, it seems—something about God Himself. It isn't enough just to believe He's God. Seems like I hardly been giving Him the time of day." He fell silent for a long time. At last he added, "I got to talk to Pa, soon as he's able. And I can't settle for bein' the way I am. I got to attend more to what the good Lord says."

"Bret."

"Yeah?"

"Micah says that there are people in the East like the grass on the prairie, and that beyond them are more places filled with countries, which all have people in them. Do you truly believe that one Great Spirit rules them alone, and that He would think of you—just you—and come to you like this?"

"Sure. That's why He's God. He rules all people and He knows all about them better than anybody else on earth."

"He is so great, yet He visits you? You and I are untried—unknown. How could such a Spirit notice us—or even speak to us? For He would be great and mighty. Such a Spirit would kill a man if He presented Himself to him."

"Well sure, if God came in all His glory. I reckon it would kill a man—never thought about that before, though. But He tells us in the Bible that He can speak to us with a still, small voice." Bret felt a little pleased at remembering this point. Joseph asked hard questions, and he wasn't sure he could answer all of them.

The blond boy, his face shadowed in the gloom of the room, looked toward the window. "I would think you mad if I had not seen these things myself," he said at last. "For I always knew that spirits ruled men more than they reckoned—yet to find that the one Great Spirit is—is like your father or the doctor or Micah—"

"They're like Him," Bret corrected.

But Joseph fell silent, and Bret wished he had held his tongue. Yet the boy was not sulking. He merely stared out the window, lost in thought.

Chapter Fifteen
Thinking of Trouble

"Pa?" Bret rested his hand on the door frame and looked anxiously at Pa, propped up on pillows and staring out the bedroom window.

"Hello, son. Come in."

"How you feeling, Pa?" Bret pulled up a wooden chair and sat down.

"More restless than a bee in a lady's bonnet. I need to be out there, Bret. There's still plenty of cowpokes and money floating around the town. There might be worse trouble yet."

"Doc and Fuller'll do a good job of watching out for things."

Pa didn't answer, only gazed restlessly around the room. "Money in the bank like that," he said at last. "All that money come in from the cattle buyers, Bret. And day after tomorrow is Sunday."

"Yeah?"

"If I was a thief and an outlaw, boy, and I had my threads runnin' through every town on the line, I reckon I'd perk my ears up at the news that there's a bank in Waterstop. And if I was to find out the sheriff was laid up, I might just wait until Sunday when nobody's about and make off with all the profits from the cattle sales.

I got to be on the street by Sunday, Bret, or it'll be other people's lives in danger—people what are paying me to watch out for 'em." Then he lay still and breathed a little bit, tired out from talking. At last he roused himself enough to say, "Well, it's in the Lord's hands. He knows I've prayed for the strength to get up and keep this town safe on the Sabbath." Pa opened his eyes and glanced sideways at Bret. "You wanted something, didn't you? What's on your mind?"

Bret felt his cheeks start to tingle. It wasn't a good time to talk about all the things going through his mind. Pa was in pain and anxious about the town. What if Pa just brushed it off? He started to shrug, but Pa's voice interrupted his excuses. "Now, son, I know you came in here for a reason. What is it? If there's something on your mind, you just tell your Pa."

Bret shrugged. "I guess I just figured you were pretty brave last night, Pa. That's all. I reckon that's all." And he started to stand up.

"Wait a minute," Pa said, and Bret sat down again. For a minute Pa looked at him steadily, and then he spoke.

"Son, I seen some rough times in my life, and I seen some good ones. I reckon last night was about one of the roughest. But when I seen you backing me up, I felt some strength come into me and I could go on. A man what's lived like I lived ain't got the right to expect his boy to turn out straight and true. But you done it, because God's done it for you. You are the best son a man could have, partner, and I reckon when the time is right you might just step into these boots, if the Lord calls you to sheriffin'. I can't think of a man better for the job, or one I'd rather hand over the badge to when I retire." And his hand grasped Bret's. "I sure want to be a good Pa to you, son. I've done you plenty of wrong in the past, but one thing that humbled me just before I was saved was seeing how I had lost your love and respect from all that I did to you. And when I see it coming back these days, I'm a mighty happy and grateful man. Come here." And Bret bent down into Pa's embrace.

Tears of relief strained to come out, but he didn't really think it fit for a man to cry, so he held them back and said, "Thanks, Pa."

Pa understood. He released him and said, "The good Lord will use you, son, wherever He sends you or whatever He tells you to do. Every day I see you having a good effect on Joseph. Seems like you were just born to make friends with people."

"Joseph asked me about God last night, Pa."

"Did he? Good. He's been so silent—hard to know when he'll answer you or when it's a good time to ask him questions. Preacher would know—oh, I forgot, Preacher's gone."

"I wonder where he went so sudden," Bret said. "Never even preached his sermon, just cleared outta' town all of a sudden."

Pa didn't answer. He was weary, and for several minutes he rested without saying anything. Then he spoke at last. "I had some bitterness in me toward Barton, Bret. The good Lord knows I can't plan to deputize a man who'll sell drink to others, but now I see I been hard on him. He's a sinner like me, just like me. And it'll take love and care to win him, just like it was love and care from you and your Ma that helped me so much."

"I reckon he was right glad to help last night."

"Yep. And in a tight corner he backed me, but I still couldn't deputize him any more, not unless we had a 'mergency like last night. Just be hypocritical to rely on the man making the whiskey that gets the other men drunk and in trouble."

"Would you have figured that when you were making moonshine?" Bret asked.

"Yeah, I think I would have. I didn't think much of the job myself, and I sure didn't expect any lawmen to like it. It was different back East, of course. Most people had the same ideas on right and wrong, even the folks doing wrong. Out here it seems like if you can back yourself up with a gun or good nerves, you're in the right."

Then they were quiet again, while Bret thought about how good it was just to sit and talk with Pa. He'd never realized how much they thought alike and agreed on things.

"Son, a town doesn't get a new bank out here without earning some trouble," Pa said. "We ain't got a decent vault, and we got a big pile of money. Doc and Fuller and some others are taking their turns watching over it, but I just know inside me that smart outlaws'll wait until the town is unprepared—Sunday afternoon, I reckon. Ain't any trains coming in until Monday morning; all the cowboys'll be back on their ranches or on the way back, and word will have it that I'm laid up."

Pa glanced sideways at Bret. "I talked to your Ma a spell last night when I couldn't sleep. I want you to pack my side gun yourself. I know you know how to use it. I hate to spend a Sunday out of the house of God, but I'm the watchman on the wall for this town, and I just know there's bad men a-comin'. We got to be prepared for them."

"Sure, Pa."

"And Doc'll fit Joseph up. I reckon he'd be good to have on hand."

"Yeah. Fact is, there won't be a regular service anyway, Pa. Preacher's gone, remember?"

"That's right." Pa's face clouded as he tried to remember something. "Seems like I saw him headin' for the cattle and the trains. Wondered where he'd be goin' in such a hurry, but I didn't get to ask him about it. Now he's gone. Hope everything's all right."

Bret stood up. Pa opened his eyes and smiled. "You might tell your Ma I'd like a sip of soup."

"Sure, Pa."

They shook hands, and Bret went out to find Ma.

Chapter Sixteen
The Vigil

Sunday morning dawned hot and dusty as midday. The sky overhead was cloudless and clear blue, like Ma's china apple bowl.

After breakfast, Pa and Bret—in their black broadcloth suits—went out to watch the street. Pa walked haltingly, and when he didn't think about it, his hand strayed over to his side. Pa said nothing about it—Bret figured he and Ma had already talked it over, and Ma knew Pa had to keep watch. He'd been up and about for two days now, but never without plenty of rest.

Just as they were going out the door, Ma looked at Bret and suddenly kissed his cheek. "You know I'll be in here prayin', son. The Lord knows I won't leave my knees until I know you're safe."

"Thanks, Ma." He'd figured he'd be embarrassed—but maybe the sound of Pa getting shot was still fresh in his mind. He leaned forward and kissed her cheek. "We'll be all right, Ma. It's just this one time."

Joseph was already gone—out to the livery stable where he would saddle up several horses and keep them fresh throughout the long day. Bret knew that on his thigh Joseph wore a six-shooter that the Doc had lent him, and on his belt he carried a hunting knife that he had borrowed from Bret.

Under the long, flapping jacket of the broadcloth suit, Bret also wore a six-shooter, and he knew that Pa had his tucked into its customary place in his waistband.

They emerged into the heat and walked silently down the creaking plank sidewalk to the sheriff's office. Pa stopped inside to get his shotgun, then rejoined Bret, and they took up their stations, Pa sitting on a stack of crates and Bret leaning against the wall alongside him. They both watched out toward the horizon line, where distant mountains were a blue blur.

Bret knew that on the other side of Main Street, Doc and Mr. Fuller were watching also. Otherwise, the street was pretty quiet.

"Maybe they got word you was up," Bret suggested after about fifteen minutes.

"Maybe," was all Pa said, and then they were quiet again.

An hour ticked by, and then another. A couple of men in workpants and wool shirts but no guns clumped down the sidewalk past them, on the way to the saloon. Pa frowned, irritated. "What this town needs is a mayor," he said. "One that'll see to it that that there place closes down at least for a Sunday. Even the hotel dining room doesn't serve food of a Sunday morning!"

"Guess a mayor's next anyway, Pa," Bret said. "Now that they got a sheriff."

"Reckon so. You know, that's a job I'd like a shot at, Bret."

Bret glanced down at him. "But you're sheriff!"

"For a year," Pa admitted. "That's what I agreed to. But it's a hard thing for a married man to wear a tin star, boy—leastways it's hard in a town like this. Most sheriffs give up the star when they get married, 'cept I was married when I got this one."

"But don't you think the Lord called you to it?"

"Sure," Pa said. Then he was silent again while anxious thoughts buzzed around in Bret's mind. Everyone was used to Pa being sheriff by this time—even Bret. Seemed like things were okay as long as Pa was around. It was hard to think of someone else being the sheriff. Then Pa spoke up again. "I reckon the Lord called me to the job, boy, but I never did ask Him if 'twere a life callin', and I don't reckon it is." He pulled out his watch and glanced at it. "Hmm, been almost two hours. Reckon we better quit jawin'. I don't really 'spect comp'ny until tonight, but we ought to be prepared in case I judged wrong."

Then they were silent again. A few more men clumped down toward the saloon—cowhands, mostly, in town on a Sunday for some reason. Some of the men and women who often gathered for services when Preacher came were out visiting—"Prayer meeting," Pa told Bret. "Ma told me last night that some of the folks were going to get together for a little service of their own. But I didn't think I ought to ask 'em to pray for this—'fraid it might have scared some of them."

Bret agreed, and watched as the bonneted women and men in broadcloth went into the front room of the barber shop. They'd likely have their prayer session upstairs, where Dave Matthews, the barber, lived with his family.

Pa looked wistful.

"Preacher does a good job, but a man could wonder why the Lord hasn't supplied more like him. Hard, dependin' on a circuit rider."

"Maybe there's some don't know they're called yet," Bret offered.

"Maybe." And once again Pa fell silent. Bret didn't pursue the conversation. He knew that Pa had once set his heart on preaching. The Lord wasn't of a mind to call him to it, though. And now there was the question of a mayor. Deep down, Bret knew that Pa would make a good one—Pa could read accounts and he couldn't be bought by anyone.

More time passed. It was getting long and dull, watching the horizon and waiting for trouble. Bret began to wish that something—anything—would happen. But nothing did. Then he got hungry. The sun was high—noontide high. Pa pulled some jerked beef out of his vest and handed it to Bret. Pa himself wouldn't even think of going home to eat dinner, and he must have figured Bret didn't want to, either.

The afternoon passed, much like the morning, with little bits of conversation and long silences made even more silent by the heat and the black broadcloth.

Pa had just put his watch back after making it to be five o'clock, when Bret spied a cloud of dust hanging over the plain.

Pa stood up, and Bret saw that he was stiff from having sat for so long. But he didn't look like he was in bad pain.

The cloud got bigger, and Bret made out five or six riders coming. Pa put his fingers in his mouth and let out two sharp whistles. Way down the street, Doc and Mr. Fuller mounted up and came riding to meet them.

"Get on the other side of the street, Bret," Pa said. "And draw your gun now. Be ready. If I let out a shot, you follow for all you're worth. These may just be drifters, but I doubt it." Bret obeyed. He crossed the wide street and ducked behind a post so that he was visible but a poor target. He kept the cool metal of the pistol grip in his hand, poised and ready to fire.

Doc and Fuller rode up and flanked Pa, one on either side of the dusty street, affording Pa lots of room but making it impossible for anyone to ride past. They had rifles across their saddles.

It was six riders, all told. They looked worn and patched like drifters, but each one sported a six-gun, and most of them had rifle sheaths on their saddles.

Pa took the shotgun in both hands and stood in the middle of the street with his feet apart. The riders came closer, closer, until Bret could make out that one had pearl-handled guns and another was wearing a sheepskin vest. They whoa'd and reined in at sight of Pa.

One fellow, a stocky hand who looked scarce older than Bret himself, spoke for the rest. "Howdy."

"Howdy," Pa said.

"This yore welcoming committee?"

"Yup. What are you boys doin', riding out in such hot weather? Ain't it your supper time?"

"We're hands lookin' for work, Sheriff. Just comin' into town to ask who's hirin'," he replied.

"Oh? Been ridin' the plains?" Pa asked.

"Shore. Gettin' on to a coupla' weeks now we been driftin'. Times is bad, and I figure there's plenty of outlaws afoot, but we don't mean no harm. We just want a bite to eat and a chance at a job."

"I reckon that's a sad enough story," Pa conceded. "'cept I don't think you're so poor you wouldn't have no bedrolls. But I don't see any. I figure you better head back to your camp and retrieve 'em. Boys as poor as you can't go leavin' your things around like that."

The lead man looked pretty sore for a minute, then he snapped, "You sayin that I'm lyin' to you, tin star?"

"I sure am." Pa leveled the shotgun. "I ain't in the mood for a gunfight, mister—I never am. I'm the sheriff of this town because I'm always prepared. One jump ahead. Now you and your boys get those horses turned around and get out of here. There's four men with drawn guns

here, against six of you a-settin' there like ducks in a gallery."

The others in the group looked around, and Bret saw one of them spot him and mumble something to the leader.

"You ain't heard the last of us, tin star!" he snapped, but he signaled for them to turn around, and they rode out until nothing was left of them but dust hanging in the air.

Chapter Seventeen
The Robbery

Pa sent Bret in for dinner after that. Along about six, Joseph came in. Bret was surprised to see the taciturn boy help Ma get dinner ready. For himself, he had two left feet in the kitchen, and he just stayed out of the way. But Joseph quietly mixed up biscuits for Ma and put them in the oven. He also took a hand keeping an eye on the big chicken that was stewing in the heavy iron pot on the stove.

"I haven't had help in the kitchen before," Ma said with a little laugh. "But you're a fair cook for your years, boy. You've been baching a long time, I suppose."

At her kind words, Joseph looked up and smiled at her. Bret figured he still didn't know what to say to Ma, or to any womenfolk, but he must have liked her, to smile so big at her. He had never smiled before.

"You gettin' used to havin' womenfolk around?" Bret asked him as they went out on the front porch to see if Pa was coming.

"White women—they are treated differently than the Indian women—" Joseph said. "I was afraid of that, you know. You cannot be very straightforward. You must treat them like they could break. But your Ma—she's been good to me. Both of your parents treat me—like a welcome guest. No, more like a person they have known forever. Do Christians—"

Whatever Joseph was about to ask was lost as a shot rang out.

"Pa!" Bret cried. His mind replayed the scene from a few days ago—Pa shot. Before he knew what was doing, he was halfway down the street, running for the bank. Joseph was at his heels. Then, just as suddenly, Joseph was gone. Bret ran on, heedlessly.

"Bret, no! Take cover!" Two more shots and Bret rolled onto the ground, took to his feet, and dodged into a doorway on the covered sidewalk.

It had been Pa calling to him—Pa was safe, then. From the cover of the doorway, Bret could see the bank. A chill ran through him. They had come back—probably one at a time, sneaking through the town during the supper hour. Perhaps they had climbed into the back of the bank— surely somebody had been on guard inside. Who? Was that who had been shot?

By instinct Bret's hand dropped to the gun at his side. But his fingers only touched the rough cloth of his trousers. The gun was gone! He had taken it off in the house. Another shot up the street warned him to stay back inside the doorway. A glance told him that several people had hurriedly thrown their shutters closed against the bullets. Otherwise the street was empty—except for him, and Pa, and the bank robbers, all hidden somewhere, but every one of them knowing where *he* was. He was pinned down.

Pa's voice bellowed across the street from a hiding place further up. "Give it up! You'll never get far from town!"

"We got someone with us, Sheriff! You jest tell yore men to back off!"

Then there was silence. Was it a bluff? Or did they really have a hostage?

"Don't put a noose around your necks!" Pa called. "If you got somebody, let him go!"

"Ain't a him, tin star—'s a little gal, an' she wants her mama. Now you and your boys pull back and we'll deliver her safe to home." Silence followed, and Bret knew that Pa was stunned by the thought of a little girl being their prisoner.

"Be awful sad to lay a white casket in the ground!" the man called out.

"All right," Pa called back. "You win. Just don't hurt her none. You'll swing for sure if you hurt her. There's not a man in the country that won't rout you out and hang you for it."

"We don't aim to hurt her—you jest come out and lay down yore gun," the voice called. "And have them other two or three fellers come out, too."

Bret could tell by then that the voice was coming out from the alley alongside the bank. So they had gotten in after all—sneaked in somehow in the last two hours and maybe climbed in through a window when whoever was on watch was eating his supper and not paying attention.

A moment later Pa's gun was tossed out from the alley by the hotel, and a moment later Pa stepped into view. Bret came out from the cover of the doorway and joined him in the street, his hands clear from his belt. Fuller came out from another doorway, threw his shotgun down, and joined them.

"Doc here?" Pa asked in a low voice.

"Takin' his supper when the shots rung out," Fuller mumbled, not looking at Pa.

"Who'd they get?"

"Jim Davis was in the bank on watch. I think they kilt him."

A bullet skidded through the dirt in front of them, kicking up spurts of dust. Bret's heart went into his throat, but he didn't flinch.

"Quit jawin', tin star!" the voice from the alley called out, irritated. "You make a good target out there!"

Pa and Fuller obeyed the command, but the voice called out again, "I say you make a good target out there!"

"I heard you," Pa said.

"You ain't very polite for a man fixin' to die."

"You can kill me, but you can't scare me, kid. You do what you've a mind to."

Bret waited, but nothing happened. After another minute or two, they heard hoofbeats on the other side of the buildings on Main Street. Pa slowly reached for his gun that was lying at his feet. Nothing happened. He scooped it up. Fuller followed suit, and they all three ran to the alleyway.

"Fuller, hoist in and check Davis," Pa ordered crisply. "Bret, go fetch Doc—" Running to the other end of the alley to find their tracks, Pa didn't stop to glance at the window, but Bret noticed that the window had been cut out, not smashed. They had entered the bank fairly silently, then.

Bret ran back out into the alley, but he heard Fuller bellow out, "Tell Doc that Davis is breathin'!"

And then he heard a little girl's cry.

Chapter Eighteen
The Chase

Bret was amazed at how quickly the town came to life. By the time Bret had Doc out on the street running for the bank, there was already a brace of men leading horses into the street—horses that backed and pulled away from the growing throng of men and women.

Pa was holding a little girl, one just old enough to be starting school. Doc rushed by the growing crowd with a brief order—"Two of you men come with me!"—and disappeared into the bank to tend after the wounded man. Two men quickly followed.

Three horses were all saddled and packed and ready, and Joseph stood by, holding the bridles of two of them with the reins of the third looped loosely on his arm. He had gone to get the horses, mindful of the job Pa had given him.

Pa passed the little girl over to one of the women. Bret recognized the child from the church service they had had several weeks back. She was from one of the smaller ranches—they must have picked her up coming back into town. But she was all right, just weepy and wanting her mama.

"The robbers were headed west by southwest," Pa said. "Goin' toward rocky country where they won't be found.

Make up a posse soon as you can, and follow us with Fuller. We'll leave sign as best we can. Hurry it up!" He glanced at Bret and Joseph. "Come on, boys!"

Bret could hardly believe it—he and Joseph would be the first to ride out with Pa! They wordlessly swung up and rode out at a gallop. With expert timing Joseph handed Bret's gunbelt over to him.

In minutes the town behind them was swallowed up in the grasslands, and they were riding toward the thick blur of mountains on the horizon.

But night was falling. They couldn't track by dusk.

A couple of times Pa swung down to check the sign, making sure that none of the robbers had veered off to lay an ambush for pursuit.

Too soon, darkness began to fall. Worse, clouds started to roll in—not storm clouds, but heavy, fluffy ones—so that there wouldn't be any stars to see by, and the moon hadn't waxed yet.

They couldn't keep the horses going at a full gallop for very long, but Pa kept the trot pretty brisk until the darkness fell completely. They came to a narrow but deep draw where a creek flowed. Then they reined in and dismounted.

"Will they have to stop, too, Pa?" Bret asked. He led the horses down and let them drink while Pa took the small blanket roll that had been strapped to his saddle.

"Maybe—if they're on treacherous ground," Pa said. "And they're headin' for the mountains—pretty much of a beeline, it looks like."

"If that's so, maybe we can follow 'em at night anyway, if you think they won't change their direction," Bret offered.

"Horses need a rest, first," Pa advised. "Let's make a hatful of fire and some coffee first. Then I believe we might ought to follow and trust that they won't veer off."

As the small campfire flared up, Joseph studied the dusky sky and tested the breeze. "Clouds might roll away," he suggested. "I don't think that they are storm clouds."

"Let's hope not," Pa agreed.

Pa put coffee on, and after it was done they gulped it in silence while the horses nibbled at little spears of muddy grass. Pa washed out the coffeepot and repacked it, then walked out of the draw to check the night sky. He came back in a few minutes. "I reckon we ought to go on at a walk, at least," he said. "We can't let them get too much of a head start on us."

They led their mounts through the shallow, cool creek and up the other side. Then they mounted up and went at a walk, letting the horses pick their way in the dimness. Pa set their course west by southwest. He was one of those unusual men who could start out on a straight line and never unconsciously veer from it. In all their misfortunes in moving west, losing their direction had never been part of their problems.

The clouds did roll back in an hour or so. But at last Pa called a halt. "If we're goin' to get anywhere tomorrow, we got to get some rest. Let's snatch a few hours' sleep."

Neither Bret nor Joseph argued. They unsaddled and let the horses roll before hobbling them. Then they settled down with blankets but no fire.

"I'll watch a bit," Pa said. "You boys get your shuteye in, and I believe I'll pray for those robbers to get tired and have to stop, too."

Joseph, about to lie down in his blanket and take advantage of the chance to sleep, stopped and looked at Pa. Bret, already on his back with one arm behind his head, glanced over at the silhouette of Joseph.

"Do you think it likely that your God will hear you?"

"I reckon so," Pa said.

"Even though I am with you?"

"What's that got to do with it?"

"I don't worship Him. I haven't, anyway."

Pa hesitated to answer, but in the silence Joseph leaned toward him. "I don't know how. How does a man approach a God like Him? He commands His followers to be kind to all, to be brave and pure and yet gentle."

"Well, you got the right idea on what He commands, Joseph. I'm glad that all them folks that called themselves Christians and treated you bad didn't convince you that they really were Christians."

"No. I know what true Christians do and believe."

"You left something out of what God commands, though, son. He commands all men, everywhere, to be saved."

"I don't know what that means."

"Do you know what repentance means?"

"No, but I've heard Micah and you say the word before."

"It means to know that you've broken the law of God and you're unfit to be in His presence, and to grieve over that and ask Him to pardon you."

"Do you mean to make myself regret wishing to kill Barton?"

"I reckon the Holy Spirit is dealing with you, now. You just put your finger on the toughest sin of your whole life, I believe—hating the folks that have been cruel to you."

"I cannot be sorry for that."

"That's because you don't know yourself how wicked your own heart is, nor what you're capable of. So you hate them because you think they're more evil than you are."

Joseph did not answer. Bret realized with a little jolt that the boy's silences had been less frequent lately. But now Joseph shut up into himself and after a minute flopped down onto the ground without speaking to Pa again.

Chapter Nineteen
Outlaw Trail

Pa rousted them before dawn. Chewing on jerked beef, they saddled up and rode with the paling eastern sky at their backs. There was no talk—each was weary from hard riding and hunger.

Though the light gradually grew better, the trail grew worse. The robbers had made no effort to hide their route, but the ground was more and more rocky.

Pa's verdict was simple. "If they aren't hiding their tracks themselves, it's because they knew all along that the trail would peter out where we couldn't find 'em."

He squinted ahead at the mountains that were much closer. "Up there. That's where they've gone, boys—knowing we'd have scant chance to find 'em."

"But Pa, some of the town men are expert trackers. Maybe they could figure out the sign."

"Maybe—there's a bunch of spurs up there. I've heard Fuller yarnin' about them over the checkerboard at the grocery. Says rustlers used to keep their goods there until they had 'em rebranded or the heat had cooled off. Accordin' to Fuller, the mountains break off into little ridges and spurs so bad that it's like tryin' to find a mouse in a maze."

"If those men were local, maybe they know the place."

Pa swung up into the saddle. "I give up my bettin' long ago," he admitted, "but if I were to bet, that's what I'd bet on. They've gone up there, too cocksure of their plan to waste time hidin' tracks or settin' up ambushes for us."

"Is it straight ahead?" Bret asked.

"That I don't know. Fuller wasn't ever real specific on its location, just told me pretty much in general terms. We got to ride up and scout, but I don't want to waste time on tracks. Let's risk everything on them being in that maze."

"You think the posse will lose us if we veer off?"

"We've got to risk it," Pa said.

"I've been this way," Joseph suddenly cut in. "Coming up with my cousin, we came this way. We came through a pass that he called a trickster. The path was hidden until we came right up on it. But I was not paying attention to the landmarks."

"Think you can find it, once we get closer?" Pa asked him.

"I can try."

"Well, let's go, then."

Bret reckoned that there wouldn't be all that many traveled passes through the mountains on the way to Waterstop. Like as not, the route Joseph took would be the same one the bandits would take.

The day before, the mountains had seemed to stay a fixed distance away—always a thick and blue blur on the horizon. But today they seemed to rush up more suddenly. In a few hours they were clattering through dry washes and old creek beds that came off the slopes.

Bret felt a little lost. He was no hand at navigating or at reading landmarks. What Pa called spurs or ridges looked like little mountains to him.

There were trees up on the mountains—aspen, spruce, and other firs clustered together in stands or running up in woody patches. But there were long bare places, too, and cluttered boulders all in heaps that spoke of avalanches back in the winter and the spring.

The ridges and the high mountains cast long shadows over them as the afternoon came on. It was a little cooler, but not much.

"Water's the key," Pa said. "They need it."

"But if they plan to keep on going, they won't have to hole up near water," Bret said. "They'll just move from place to place."

"But they will hole up, Bret. It isn't like the western dime novels anymore where a man robs a bank and rides five hundred miles to have his fling. We got the trains, now, and those boys know that news of the robbery's going to get around too fast for them to spend the money up and get off scot free. They've got to hole up until it all blows over and nobody'll put two and two together when they start spendin'."

All this time Joseph had been looking around, seeking familiar landmarks.

"Recognize anything?" Pa asked.

"No."

"What do you vote for, south down the ridges, or up higher?"

"South. When my cousin brought me to Waterstop, we crossed through the mountains and then spent several days on the grassland. We must have come through further down."

"Okay, let's scout down further. Keep your hands ready and your minds sharp. If those boys notice we're right onto them, they won't like it," Pa said.

Chapter Twenty
The Secret Pass

Another night and a fruitless day passed at the foot of the great mountains. No posse coming from behind and no sign of the outlaws ahead—nor any sign of the pass, either, Bret thought, irritated with the calmness of Joseph and Pa as they patiently searched through the myriad of stubborn rocky spurs and false ravines, looking for something Joseph could recognize. Two days in the saddle wore Pa out, and he rode with a hand to his side but said nothing about the pain. And nobody said anything about being hungry, but Bret thought a lot about it.

Even at night there was no sign of anything, no telltale smoke or fire's glow.

The afternoon was on the wane on the second day when Joseph came riding out from behind a stand of trees.

"A path! A path! I think I've found it!"

Pa and Bret were too tired to say anything; they only followed hard after him, past the trees, across a brook that still had some water in it, and down into deep ravine.

It looked doubtful to Bret, a deep gap in the earth, widening until it terminated at a granite wall. This wall rose up maybe fifty feet above the ground. It was the end of a spur off a larger mountain.

Nevertheless, they rode down to the face of rock, and just as Bret was about to rein in with disgust, he saw the abrupt turnoff behind a stack of rocks.

The small pile of rocks itself was a giveaway—they had been piled in too orderly a way to be a work of nature. Man had done it. It was a landmark, a signal to someone that the route lay this way.

"He called this the staircase," Joseph said, still excited. "See how it climbs onto a steep part of the mountain. Come on!"

In single file the horses walked up the steep path that corkscrewed along the mountain on one side and was sheltered by trees on the other. At last they came out into the open, much higher up than they had been.

Bret could see the tops of other mountains in the distance, though he knew he was on the mere kneecap of this one. The path leveled out, and they followed over grassy places and then down a ridge again.

All this while the afternoon was dying away. In places where there was rock or trees on the west side, they rode in twilight, and they would emerge into daylight in clearer places. It was in the light that Pa stopped suddenly and pointed to a softer place where water had run off recently from a rainstorm.

"Look."

It was a single hoofprint, cast firmly in the mud, and not more than two days old.

Gradually the pass widened out. The ground became pretty level when they went to the feet of the mountains again. Now they were among the mountains instead of lingering on their skirts. Decent daylight was cut off. Though the sky way above was still pale blue, shades of deep blue, violet, and gray had fallen among the ridges, gullies, ravines, and on the path itself—shadows cast by the trees or an early night thrown down from the mountains themselves. They rode up between the high rock walls on either side until they came out again at a level place. The trail ahead of them went upwards into trees, and along their right side another steep slope ran up the mountain. To their left the downward slope was more gradual, dipping down through several patches of trees and then ending in a sheer cliff. The slopes and ridges above were pretty, but Bret didn't hanker for a climb in the twilight.

Pa reined in. "Let's stop where it's level for a space and we've got some shelter. No fire again, I'm afraid."

It was a dry camp again, with only jerked beef and hard biscuit to eat, and not much of that, this late into the search.

Lying on his back, Bret watched the starry sky. He wondered where the posse was. Could they even depend on the posse now? It had been hard enough for them to get back on the right track, and that was only because Pa had made the correct assumption that the outlaws would head for this pass so far to the south. What if the posse figured they went north to an easier pass? Even if the posse did guess right, it would be hard for them to find the pass itself. It had taken Pa and Joseph two days, and Joseph had been this way once before.

"Sssh, boys—" it was Pa.

Bret sat up. Joseph was sitting, too, looking at Pa. Pa gestured upward to where one of the many ridges rose above them. Bret looked up, scanning the rock and the sky.

When he saw it, he jumped a little bit—a glow, regular and steady, shining like a yellow star. It was not a fire, but a lamp, a lamplight in a glass chimney that had been set too close to a window.

"That's them above us," Pa whispered. "They must figure we lost 'em bad. They ain't keepin' watch or they'd a' shot at us by now."

"Why didn't we see their cabin?" Bret whispered.

"Trees," Joseph whispered. "Their shack is surrounded by trees, but the lamplight is still visible—"

"—like a beacon," Pa added. "Come on. The Lord's protected us in our ignorance, but we better get under good cover with the horses."

They stood up and silently gathered their camp things together. In a few minutes they had led the horses further down the way they had come, behind a stand of trees.

They hobbled the horses again and sank down in different places behind the trees. Up ahead and above was the cabin, to the right was the path and a high, tree-covered slope. To the left of the stand of trees, the ground sloped down and then abruptly dropped off in a cliff.

"First watch, Bret," Pa called over in a whisper.

"Sure, Pa."

Down here, lower on the ridge, they couldn't see the lamplight anymore, but Bret stretched out on his stomach behind a tree with the blanket bundled up under his chest so he could lean his elbows on it and watch for intruders.

Now what? he asked himself. Nobody knew where the posse was, and that meant the posse sure didn't know where they were. And there were at least six outlaws to the band of three trackers. Yet Pa must bring the robbers to justice. Maybe he would send somebody back to find the posse, or maybe he'd think of some way to trick the outlaws into surrender. For the first time in two days, he thought about Ma. If something happened to Pa or to himself, or to both of them, who would take care of Ma? Now he understood why Pa didn't think it was easy for a married man to be a sheriff—it was hard on the womenfolk, all right!

Chapter Twenty-one
Pinned Down

Bullets rattled and kicked up the dust in a neat half-circle around the saddle under Pa's head.

At the very first shot Bret had rolled down around the roots of the aspens around him and drawn his six-shooter.

Pa leaped clear while a bullet kicked right between his heels. Two of the horses neighed and tried to break off their hobbles. They fell and rolled, screaming in the terrible way that only horses can scream. Hunched under the boughs of a massive pine, Pa deftly reached out into the danger area and snaked his rifle out of the sheath where it lay alongside the saddle.

Joseph, already in a low furrow of the ground and protected by big heavy roots, had his six-gun in his hand. The shots weren't coming from the cabin but from the other side of them, raining down from the slope above on the other side of the path. The evening before, the slope had seemed nothing more dangerous than a place where water would run off in a storm, but now Bret saw it for what it really was—a vantage point behind the outlaws' cabin where men could station themselves and hail down gunshot or even rocks on enemies coming up the pass.

The terrain on Bret's side of the pass sloped gradually down but stopped sharply with a sheer drop-off farther down. No escape there.

The truth hit Bret all of a sudden: they were trapped, high ground in front of them and an eventual drop-off behind them. And two of them had nothing more than handguns to fight a pitched battle. Suddenly everything was reversed—they were no longer in pursuit but were pursued.

Pa drew out his six-gun and laid the rifle aside. Bret guessed the plan—try to make them think they had no rifles, get them to close in.

After a minute another volley of shots made them keep their heads down. Bret saw one of their attackers bob up more boldly and shoot with a rifle.

"Boys, you watch the path to the cabin," Pa ordered. "Don't let them take us on the flank!"

"Right, Pa."

Bret turned his attention to the way they had retraced the night before. Almost as Pa feared, a new volley of bullets hailed down from there and ricocheted among the rocks.

"It's the ricochets that might do us in," Pa mumbled. The one man he had sighted took the trouble to take a more deliberate aim at the horses. Pa snatched up the rifle, and just as the outlaw fired, Pa fired.

"One less," Pa said grimly. "But he put my horse away."

One man by the cabin path would leap up, fire off a shot, drop down, and then reappear in a different spot and fire.

"That's an Indian trick, ain't it?" Bret asked Joseph. There was no answer, and Bret glanced over. Joseph was gone!

"Pa—" but then he caught himself. There was nothing Pa could do. Joseph had left his gunbelt and .45 in easy reach of Bret, and Bret took up the spare gun.

Then he saw Joseph, the blond head popped up behind a tree much further up, behind the man that was so determinedly stalking down toward Bret with a rifle. Indian fighting!

"Feller, you picked the wrong boy to play Indians with," Bret murmured. "You're takin' on the real thing."

In another instant the outlaw's head and gun popped up again, but before he got a shot off, there was a blur of Joseph's knife and then Joseph himself darted across the path and leaped atop the fallen man. They spilled out onto the path, both pitifully exposed to gunfire from either side, and then they rolled against a tree on the near side of the path that sheltered them from above. The outlaw, bigger, older, more murderous than Joseph, had been hit in the shoulder by the knife. There was blood down his back and on his arm as he wrestled with Joseph for the rifle.

He freed his bad arm to cuff Joseph's face, and though the blow landed, Joseph didn't flinch but rather yanked the rifle away with a sweep and used it as a club in those close quarters to knock the man down. Then he disappeared over the edge of the slope on Bret's side. A few minutes later he came puffing up the steep slope from behind the stand of trees and rejoined his friends.

"Two rifles, Sheriff."

Pa glanced at him. "Where'd you—" But gunfire made him turn back.

"That fellow still alive?" Bret asked.

"Plenty alive." Joseph ruefully rubbed his jaw. "Just unarmed and very angry. Your God would not want me to kill him unless I had to."

"You're right, He wouldn't."

114

"But the man cannot fight any more. Now it is four of them against the three of us. Better, eh?" Joseph asked.

"Better," Pa agreed, "except we're sitting here in a trap. They've still got a king-sized upper hand judgin' from the point of view of strategy. We're pinned down and they're sittin' pretty."

"If only one of us could get up that slope behind them," Bret wished. "He could even the odds up there."

"Doesn't seem possible," Pa said. "There's no covered way to get up there from here."

"Well, maybe we can hold them off until help comes," Bret suggested. "Or maybe we could trick them into doing something foolish."

"The posse might come," Joseph added.

"If they're close enough to hear the shots," Bret agreed, but in his heart he knew how remote those chances were. The posse could be anywhere.

"We got to pray that if the posse does come they don't rush into gunfire," Pa added. "That path is mighty exposed, and some of the men'll be picked off before they reach cover. Those outlaws are crafty. It's no wonder they didn't care about the lamp in the window. Nobody could come close without them hearin' it, and they knew that at first light they would be able to see if anyone was on their trail." Pa looked grim. "We got to think of something, boys, and we got to do it before dark comes."

Chapter Twenty-two
Unto the Hills

Hours ticked by. Occasional shots whizzed back and forth, but the volleys from the morning were never repeated. Sometimes somebody tried to sneak down along the path, but Bret or Joseph was always prompt to drive him back, and—since Joseph's exploit of the morning—the outlaws seemed wary.

In the daylight they would be wary, anyway, but Bret knew that as soon as night fell the outlaws could take better positions and surround the sheriff's band.

As shadows from the slope across from them gradually fell across the patch of trees where they hid, Bret considered making another plea with Joseph about his soul. The Indian-raised boy had little enough fear of death—more the pity, for he could very well plunge unafraid into hell, a thought that Bret could not bear.

It ain't dying that's hard, he thought, it's knowing Joseph's lost. He's never had a friend in his life 'cept for Christians, and now he's at least interested in the Bible and the gospel, and it looks like he's going to die just a few hours short of repenting and being converted. But then, maybe he won't die here. After all, God rules all men, and He's the one that put Joseph in that fellow Micah's way and then in ours.

Bret never knew when he switched from thinking to praying about Joseph's life, but half an hour went by while he watched the path with one eye and prayed in the meantime.

It was more shots from above that roused him.

"They have moved higher on the slope," Joseph said. "Why?"

But suddenly they saw one of their attackers fall away from behind a tree where he had been crouched.

"That man's been hit—" Pa began.

"The posse?" Bret asked. "Up there?"

"Impossible, the posse'd have to come from the other way."

They watched the wooded slope above them. More shots, then a shout: "Throw down your guns, bandits! We got you nailed in!"

Joseph's head came up. His eyes glistened. Bret glanced at him. "Micah!" he exclaimed. "That was Micah!" The blond boy nearly stood, but Bret and Pa pulled him down. "You sit tight or Micah will be coming back to your funeral!" Pa exclaimed.

"How can you say that? Haven't we prayed for it? Don't you believe your God anymore? He's brought Micah back!"

"He must be alone," Pa mused. "Unless he came with the posse. He could have led 'em around in a circle to come in behind the outlaws."

"Yes, Micah could. He knows the mountains well," Joseph affirmed.

"But he might have come by himself if he came too late to catch the posse," Bret said. It didn't matter. Even one lone man, perched on the top of the slope, reversed the entire situation for the trapped men, and it tipped the numbers in their favor.

A man from the slope came out with his hands raised and stood on the path.

"I've got you covered," Pa called. "Where are the others?"

"Only two left—up at the cabin," he said, keeping his hands high.

In another minute or so, two men came down the path, hands up, followed at gunpoint by a man Bret had never seen before, and behind him, Preacher!

Pa stood up, keeping his rifle on their prisoner, but his eyes flitted over to Preacher.

"That's where he went, then," he mumbled. "To get Micah for Joseph."

"God must have told him so, after I prayed," Joseph added. "And made him find Micah."

"I reckon so," Pa agreed.

The light skin of Joseph's face had gone chalky white at sight of Micah. Micah quietly bunched the three men together, and Pa covered them. Joseph and Bret came out from the trees in time to hear Preacher say, "There's one fellow up there with a hurt shoulder that I'll look after. Looks like he's been lyin' there all day."

"I reckon I know who did that to him," Micah said. He was a lean man, several years younger than Pa, with more than a few days' growth on his face but soft blue eyes and something that suggested book learning. Joseph looked at him, but said nothing.

"What's the matter?" Bret whispered to Joseph. "Ain't you glad to see him?" But Joseph kept his eyes fixed on Micah. Micah turned to look at him and held out his hand.

"Howdy, partner."

Joseph reached to take the hand and suddenly Micah pulled him into a rough bear hug and said, "We'll go back to the mountain soon, if you want. Everything's all right now."

"Micah—Micah—" and Joseph started to cry. Bret gaped at him, until a nudge from Pa brought him back to his manners. They herded the outlaws back toward the cabin to look for rope to tie them with.

It took a couple of hours to bind the prisoners, build a litter for the injured man, who had already taken fever from lying in the dirt with his wound unbound, and bury the other two.

Preacher read Scripture over the graves—"The way of the transgressor is hard"—and preached a little; then he added, "A Christian man is always sorry to kill another man, for any reason, but no Christian can allow any man to terrorize or wrong the innocent. These men were slaves of their greed and passion and hatred, and they have yielded their lives up to these cruel masters. So let us take heed of who has the rule over us." Then he prayed, and afterward they put their hats on, helped the prisoners mount, put the injured man in the litter between two horses, and mounted up.

"Reckon we'll meet that posse on the way back," Micah said with a snort. He had told Pa and Bret his story. Preacher had seen Joseph in the town and had ridden off to find Joseph's cousin and had heard the whole story— how the gold had been lost and Joseph was working to earn the money to leave and find Micah. Preacher had ridden out to find Micah and had brought him back just as the posse was starting out. He and Micah had joined the posse, and Micah, who knew the mountains, had guessed the exact place where the outlaws would go, but nobody would listen to him.

He and Preacher had ridden out by themselves and circled around the long way to come up the back way on the cabin. They had come upon the desperate situation of the sheriff's men just in time.

"You are a fair shot with a rifle," Pa told Micah as they went down the path on their horses.

"With a rifle, yes, but I'm no account with a six-shooter. Never did work with one much. But I carry the rifle on a shoulder strap and can pretty much swing it up for quick use if I have to."

"I'm thinking of turnin' in my badge at the end of the year," Pa told him. "Be right nice to have you take the job."

Micah laughed and glanced back at Joseph. "My partner there would probably like that, but it would mean settling in town with no job in the meantime."

"You got education?"

"Sure. Worked for the railroad awhile, until the paperwork got to me."

"Maybe you could teach school next term while I finish out. We need a teacher, too."

"That's a point—I'd like to get Joseph into a regular school for a while. I taught him to read some and he tells me the town doctor's been helping him, too."

"I didn't know that," Pa said. Micah lagged behind and let the Preacher and Joseph and the prisoners get further ahead.

"Maybe he was shy about it. I guess that cousin of his took him where folks were hard on him again. They probably called him stupid and backward like mean folks will. I was a fool to hand him that money in plain sight of his cousin—should have known it would have been too big a temptation. All it did was put the boy right back into slavery, practically."

Bret couldn't help interrupting. "What did he say about the Lord? Anything? He'd told us he'd asked God to bring you back to him."

"He asked me to forgive him for leaving so sudden. That's a big step for a boy who's been raised to look out for himself. The Indians, you know, they don't think of sin as sin, not like we do. I think he's close to knowing the Lord. His heart's mighty restless, I know that much."

Chapter Twenty-three
Sheriff at Waterstop

A haze of dust still settled so slowly over the street that it seemed like a curtain hanging in the air. Bret stood out on the front walk, waiting for Pa to come back. He'd been meeting with the town council, talking with them about a mayor for Waterstop.

Bret felt a little sad. Whether the council decided to elect a mayor or not, Pa had promised Ma that he would give up sheriffing after the year was up. He didn't think the Lord had it for him to do anymore.

"Maybe my job was just to bring Joseph to town," Pa had told him. "Because that was the first step for Joseph to find Micah again. If he'd been trapped on that ranch as a mariann, he'd have never seen Preacher, and Preacher wouldn't have known to go after Micah."

It sounded like maybe it was so. Bret himself had promised Ma that he'd never be sheriff, either. He'd learned up on the mountain that he didn't want to spend his days chasing outlaws and shooting back and forth with them. Deep down he knew that God would never call him to the job.

His thoughts were interrupted by Joseph's stepping down from the plank sidewalk and coming up the walk to the house. The boy had new clothes that Micah had bought for him. These days he was walking with his head a little higher, and whenever Bret saw him and Micah on the street together, Joseph would be talking in conversation with the man, free and easy like any other boy. One week had worked big changes.

"I'm glad to find you alone," Joseph said. It was unusual for him to start a conversation. And Bret felt some surprise at the directness of his statement.

"What's on your mind?" Bret asked.

"I've been proud, sometimes, and angry. And I've gotten you into trouble—the time I threw the sickle at Barton, and you fought to help me. Now I am a Christian, too, and I have turned away from these things."

Bret straightened up in surprise at the quiet announcement, but after a moment all he said was, "I could sort of see that the good Lord was workin' on you."

Joseph smiled. "I see it now, but I didn't then. Micah said it gave him a sweat to think of me being shot at and knowing I hadn't made my peace with God."

"Him and me, both," Bret agreed. "But while I was praying for you, I saw better what—"

"You prayed for me?"

"Sure! We were on the edge of gettin' killed!"

Joseph nodded. "I must see your Ma and thank her. She prayed for us, too. And she has been good to me." He gave Bret a half-smile. "And after that, Micah says we must see Barton—to apologize first; then perhaps we can see about the money that was lost."

Bret's eyebrows went up, but he didn't push the subject of Barton. He only gestured to the house. "Ma's inside. Go on in, but, say—" Bret stopped him again. "Micah make up his mind about sheriffin' next year?"

Joseph grinned again. "He wants to. He wants me to work for him someday! If I do well in school."

Bret nodded and watched in the growing twilight as Joseph stumped up to the house in his big boots to pay respects to Ma. He turned back and saw Pa coming, way up the street. Pa waved, a dusty silhouette on the street. It looked like the news was good. Bret hurried out of the yard and strode up onto the sidewalk to meet him.